# SOUTHFI

## WEBO

Stephen Baxter was b
attended Cambridge Univ........ he has
worked in engineering, teaching and computing.
He has had several adult science-fiction novels
published by HarperCollins.

Other titles in the
THE WEB series

**GULLIVERZONE**

**DREAMCASTLE**

**UNTOUCHABLE**

**SPIDERBITE**

**LIGHTSTORM**

**SORCERESS**

**CYDONIA**

**COMPUTOPIA**

**SPINDRIFT**

**WALKABOUT**

**AVATAR**

**SERIES EDITOR**
Simon Spanton

For more information about the books,
competitions and activities, check out our website:
http://www.orionbooks.co.uk/web

# THE WEB
## WEBCRASH

◆

## STEPHEN BAXTER

Dolphin Paperbacks

*To Sophie Williams*
*and*
*Tom and Lizzie Smart*

First published in Great Britain in 1998
as a Dolphin paperback
by Orion Children's Books
a division of the Orion Publishing Group Ltd
Orion House
5 Upper St Martin's Lane
London WC2H 9EA

A catalogue record for this book is available
from the British Library
Typeset by Deltatype Ltd, Birkenhead, Merseyside
Printed in Great Britain
ISBN 1 85881 632 7

# CONTENTS

# PROLOGUE

Hi. My alias is Metaphor. I'm female, 15 years old, and I live in England Canton, British Province, European Union. The date is February 12, 2028.

I'm going to tell you a story.

Some of it is what happened to me. Some of it I put together later from what people told me and what I found out when I browsed the Web. You may not believe it. Sometimes I'm not sure I believe it all myself. But it's the truth as I lived it.

Read this and tell people about it.

Because I believe we are – all of us, all over the world – in great danger.

The Web isn't a game any more.

# CHAPTER ONE

# WEBCRASH

Of course you remember the WebCrash.

Everybody remembers the WebCrash. What were you doing that day?

I was cruising through n-space in a two-person spaceship called *The Empress's Mighty Fist*. I was working as a Browser in the Galaxias Domain – or specifically as a Pilot in that imaginary future – with one of the universe's greatest criminals as my sole companion.

Nothing too unusual about that, of course. Just school-work.

But then all the stars went out – and came back on again, subtly changed.

I didn't know about the WebCrash at the time. All I knew was I got a Web warning about a possible Domain breach, and there was a jolt as our ship dropped into real space like a snowflake falling on velvet.

I lay in my contoured Pilot's couch and tried to settle my beating heart.

It had already been a bad day. There had been rogue currents in n-space. Dealing with them while trying to keep a track on the telepathic Beacons that guided me through n-space, had left me with a headache. But now the pressure was fading. I reached under my control helmet and wiped salt sweat from my eyes.

A voice growled from the rear of the bridge. 'By the Plutonium Throne, what's going on?'

I swivelled my couch and pushed the helmet from my

head. The platinum globe floated patiently into the air.
'Numinus,' I said. 'I guess that woke you up.'

'Too right, it did.' Numinus Torca, fallen heir to the
Plutonium Throne, was a squat, dark man. Now, his
bearded face was a scowling mask. I noticed a rim of skin
armour at the neck of his towelling robe. Numinus didn't
trust anybody any more – not even me!

I was a real person, of course, playing a role in the
Domain. But Numinus wasn't real. Like the rest of the
Domain, he was generated by the computer banks that
create Galaxias.

Of course he *thought* he was real.

The bridge of *The Empress's Mighty Fist* was a squat
cylinder. I lay at its heart surrounded by banks of displays
(although, of course, I was really lying at home in our spare
bedroom wearing my new Websuit). Now Numinus
clumped to the centre of the bridge and peered about at the
monitors. 'Pilot,' he said menacingly. 'I see stars I don't
recognize. What's more, I don't see the planet Raq. We
weren't due to leave n-space again until we made Raq, were
we?'

N-space is a kind of parallel space which lets you take
short-cuts to the stars.

I took a deep breath. 'I'm sorry,' I said. 'We're not there
yet. Obviously. I had to break the journey.'

The Regent's eyes were small, dominated by huge,
piercing pupils – and he was staring at me so hard he was
frightening me more than usual.

'We hit a rogue current,' I said. 'I nearly lost control. At
the end, I lost the Beacons and got dumped back into real
space.'

'Metaphor, you're telling me things I don't want to
know,' Numinus said softly. 'I've got to get to Raq. My Lord
Silvre waits there. I must contact him and perhaps bring
him back to serve the Empire.' In fact, he meant to ask
Silvre – another crook – to help him wage war against
Numinus's mother, Empress of the Galaxy. 'That is my

mission. You've been instructed to take me to Raq. That is your mission. Now, I suggest we resume our journey.'

Numinus couldn't hurt me, of course. Nothing can really hurt you in the Web (or so they promise you!). Even so, he was a *scary* man, and I shuddered. But I had to speak up.

'I don't think you understand, Regent. N-space is not an easy ocean to sail. If we get caught in that current again we could find ourselves swept outside the Galaxy. And the route we follow may close within minutes behind us, never to reopen.'

I was serious about this. We had to be careful. For a Domain like Galaxias, a Breach would be the worst possible disaster. But Numinus wasn't supposed to know about it, because he wasn't real, and he wasn't supposed to know *that*.

Numinus fumed, and stalked around the cabin, as I tried to find a way out of this mess.

If you're lucky you won't have ever visited a Domain.

Every Domain is contained in Webtown, which is inside the Web, a huge electronic universe maintained by a worldwide network of computers. You spin into it, from home, or school, or a private booth, by wearing a Websuit that makes you feel as if you're *there*. But if you don't know any of *that* you probably won't be reading this story anyway.

Anyhow, you'll find Domains in the Library Block of Webtown. They are artificial realities. When you're in there you feel as if you're in a whole new world.

Everywhere you reach inside the Web is artificial, generated by computers. You may feel as if you're walking on the Moon, or swimming in the Caribbean, or fighting giant crocodiles in the Cretaceous Era. Whatever. But, actually, you are just lying at home, or school, or in a private booth, in a Websuit, and the suit creates the illusion of a different world for you.

But most Web environments are obvious fakes: game

zones like the DreamCastle, or entertainment zones like Cydonia, or theme parks like GulliverZone. Most Web environments are like cartoons. They are based on Realworld, and they do resemble it a bit, but they aren't meant to be exactly like it.

Domains are a little different.

Domains *are* supposed to be accurate – at least as much as their designers and people from the universe and research institutes can make them.

You may have heard of WebMars, where NASA and the Japanese and European space agencies have people trying to survive in a colony at the Martian South Pole. The idea is that if you can figure out how to do it in the safety of a Domain – from which you can be retrieved in an instant – you can then go on to apply those lessons to living on the real Mars.

And then there's WebJurassic, where researchers have built up a complete model of the Jurassic era, when, as even bratty kids like my brother George will know, dinosaurs ruled the Earth. The world back then was a complex place, and the only way the scientists can work out how all the different pieces fit together – the plants, the climate, the animals – is by creating a copy of the world (a piece of it anyhow) and letting it run.

There are even worlds that couldn't exist, such as WebRaft, where the force of gravity – which is what makes us stick to the Earth – is made much stronger. Everything's different there. Stars are only a kilometre wide and burn out in a year, and the people live on a big raft floating on air. The scientists go (in their Websuits) and live there, trying to see what it would be like to live in such a different universe.

Domains are supposed to be *pure*. There isn't supposed to be any leakage from Realworld or from other Domains. Apart from the Search Engines, there is supposed to be no way to move from one Domain to another.

That's the theory.

Another thing about Domains is the people.

In a Domain you'll meet *real* people. You might meet King Henry VIII, for instance. Some of these are avatars – characters being role-played by human beings in Websuits, who might come from anywhere in Realworld. But most of the people are phaces – artificial people generated inside the Web itself.

In the rest of the Web, the phaces are usually just dummies, with no more intelligence than a toaster. But to make domains authentic, most of the phaces are self-aware – that means they think and feel, like you and me. And the most important thing is, *they don't know their Domain is fake*.

So if you meet a Henry VIII phace, you're meeting a computer creation who thinks he is the *real* Henry. And you'd better curtsy or bow! And don't forget how much computing power it's all taking.

The bad news is that a lot of Domains allow in young people to work as Browsers. In fact they encourage it. You might get to live as a servant at the court of King Henry VIII for a week, for instance, and learn all about what life was like in the sixteenth century. You get a special Websuit which lets you transmit your experiences around the Web for the benefit of others (which is why you're called a Browser).

It's all grittily realistic (there's no TV and you work at menial jobs from dawn to dusk) and authentic (you have the basic Web safety equipment, like scuttle-buttons to get out, and are bound by the usual rules – no more than a few hours in the Web at any one time, to avoid Websickness – but otherwise it's exactly like the sixteenth century or whenever: shirts of sack cloth instead of modern custom gear, *so* cog).

All this is a *Learning Experience*.

Parents and teachers are strangely keen on stays in Domains – as opposed to, say, the Web gaming zones. If you want to find a Domain look up *educational* and cross-index *uplifting* and *morally improving*, file under *good for young people*.

Yep, most Domains are dull, dull, dull.

Anyway, back in January – when the Christmas school holiday still had six more weeks to run – right on schedule, Philip (that's my dad) started telling me I should do *something more useful with my time than spinning into the Web gaming zones and chat rooms*. And I knew I was in trouble. When he said he had a reward for me after the way I handled my perilous time in Gulliverzone (which is another story!) I knew the trouble was serious.

The *reward* was that he had fixed up for me to go work as a Browser in the Domain of my choice. He even had a new Browser Websuit for me. It looked like a scuba-diving suit, in a pastel colour so washed-out and old-fashioned it wouldn't even have been cool in the Millennium Dome.

A Domain would be *fun*, Philip said, and *educational* as well.

As if two days a week of school, for fifteen weeks of the year, isn't enough!

He was decent enough to give me a choice of which Domain I would be sentenced to. I spent a couple of hours in a Search Engine checking out the options. Search Engines, the only way to travel between the Domains, are fun. You can see out but you're invisible to the inhabitants of the Domain. It's a little like riding a glass-bottomed boat and staring at the fish under the sea.

I could go visit WebVin – a Domain dedicated to recreating life in the Viking era, circa AD 973. Or I could spend more time in Galaxias – an interstellar empire of the year AD 3000, one of the few Domains set in the future.

In WebVin, I found, mostly you get to bake bread. The life of the Vikings was *not* as glamorous, most of the time, as you might think.

I opted for Galaxias.

Philip didn't exactly approve of Galaxias. It's known as a tough, dangerous place. Very adult. He wanted me to go back on the Search Engine and find somewhere, as he put it, *nicer*. Happily for me I couldn't have gone in again if I'd wanted to, which I didn't, because the Search Engine crashed (and I would find out more about that later).

I spent a last few days spinning in and out of the Web with my friends, cramming in as much fun as I could before facing the mind-numbing boredom of the Domain. At least, I *thought* it would be boring. And then I put on my new Browser's Websuit, prayed that nobody would see me in it, and spun into Galaxias.

And that was where I was when the WebCrash hit.

The Regent bunched a fist and studied it thoughtfully. 'I've been patient enough, Metaphor. Try to take this in. All this is your problem. Just get me to Raq.'

I was getting a little tired of Numinus's bullying and threats. The fact is I was trying to save him.

If a Domain Breach happens – two Domains cross over because of some hardware failure – any characters who become aware of the existence of the Web outside their world, or of any other Domains, are supposed to be shut down. It seems a little harsh (though I wouldn't have shed any tears over Numinus), but that is the protocol.

I was actually trying to protect Numinus from being shut down.

Not that he would have appreciated it.

I pushed more strength into my voice. 'And I'm telling you, Numinus, we can't return to n-space until—' Until the warnings of a Domain Breach stopped, but I couldn't tell him that. 'Until the storm in n-space disperses.'

'How long?'

I shrugged. 'Three or four days?'

'One day.' Numinus threw a fast punch at my control helmet. The sphere rocked in the air. 'We resume our journey in one day. Is that clear?'

'Oh, get off my bridge, Numinus,' I said tiredly.

For now, I'd had enough. Out of his sight I punched my scuttle-button and got out of there.

Scuttling out of Domains is a bit complicated.

If anybody from Realworld is in a Domain, time in the Domain carries on at a normal pace. But if nobody is there, the Domain might freeze – or it might fast-forward, like a video. The phaces aren't aware of this, of course. It doesn't matter to them that a year in the Domain might go by so fast that it only takes a second of Realworld time, or be slowed down so it takes a decade. To them, it *feels* like a full year of their lives.

Anyhow, as far as Numinus was concerned, I would simply fall asleep. If I chose not to return at all I would be replaced by another phace, a placeholder that wouldn't be self-aware.

But I wasn't thinking about any of this technical stuff at the time. Because when I opened my eyes, I was lying on my back in the cosy warmth of our spare bedroom – and the walls were flashing warning red!

# CHAPTER TWO

# NORRLAND

What I didn't know, couldn't know yet, was that the WebCrash was global. It affected every corner of Realworld, and all the virtual worlds of the Web too.

Later, I would find out what happened in the Domain called WebVin, from the point of view of a phace called Thyri who knew nothing about Realworld and Domain Breaches.

To Thyri, the only reality was WebVin, and she thought her world was coming to an end.

AD *973: Norrland, the coast of Sweden.*

There was a wind from the north.

Thyri pulled the cart off the road from Helgo, and let the pair of horses slow to a stop.

The wind was thin, cold as a knife in the flesh.

Thyri shivered, and not just from the cold. *Valkyries abroad*, she thought.

The horses snickered uneasily, tossing their heads. Thyri reached forward and patted their rumps. 'I know,' she said. 'I know.'

Huddled against his wife, Gunnar was a sleeping bundle on the seat beside Thyri. The old Viking warrior stirred and stretched, his ice-blond hair shining in the starlight. The bandage around his eyes was grimy again, she noticed.

'Thyri? Where are we? What's wrong?'

'We're an hour from home.' Thyri said gruffly. 'There's nothing wrong. I didn't mean to wake you.' She tried a laugh. 'I need you to get your sleep and build up your strength.' She looked back at the rolls of pig-iron, the kegs of saltpetre that lay in silent heaps in the rear of the cart. 'When we get home you've got to help me shift this lot.'

Gunnar turned his sightless head. 'Well, if nothing's wrong, why did we stop?'

'I ...'

The northern wind rose again. It swept across the Norrland coastal plain, rustling the pine trees and whispering in the heather that clung to the bare rock.

A comforting lie died on Thyri's lips. There was something coming in that wind, she sensed. Something deadly: the wind was the call of the Valkyrie, the flying goddesses who select those to be slain in battle.

(It was, in fact, the noise of the Domain Breach, but Thyri couldn't know that. Not yet!)

'Thyri?'

She clutched her husband. 'There's nothing to be frightened of.'

But was that true?

The horses skipped restlessly.

Gunnar stirred sleepily. 'Thyri, can we go home now? I feel cold.'

He sounded very old, she thought.

In the Valkyrie wind, she held Gunnar's face. Her hands, scarred as they were by long years of working metal, were like bits of battered wood. 'Yes, of course.' Thyri took the reins, unease still prickling at her mind.

The cart bumped back onto the rustled track. Gunnar snuggled into his cloak once more.

Thyri tried to understand what was happening. Suppose this deep fear she felt was more than just fancy. Suppose her instinct was responding to something real. What could be the source of peril? And why should she feel personally threatened?

She could think of only one reason.

'Gunnar.' Gently, she nudged her husband awake again.

'Hmm?'

'Do you still have the Key?'

Gunnar said, 'Of course I have the Key. It's at home.'

'Where?'

'I don't know. I think it's under my pallet.'

The Key was a mysterious object from the east. Gunnar had brought it back from his last battle in Byzantium. But Gunnar had paid a heavy price for his trophy. Savage bandits from those parts, intent on stealing the Key, had captured Gunnar and plucked out his eyes before he fought his way out.

The Key had cost Gunnar his sight, and when he brought it home Thyri had loathed it immediately.

Somehow, she intuitively knew the Key was the centre of the disquiet she felt now.

All these memories, of events years before, were real to Thyri and Gunnar. But the Domain had only been operating for a few months. In Realworld time Gunnar's trip to the east might have taken place only *hours* before. Domains are strange places if you think about them too hard.

Thyri said, 'Gunnar, I want you to do something for me. First thing in the morning, take that Key out and bury it.'

'What?'

'Take a spade, go as far as you can from the house, and bury it. As deep as you can.'

'But ...' Puzzlement creased Gunnar's round face. 'Why? Why now? You know what it means to me—'

'I don't want to discuss it,' Thyri snapped. 'You don't have to get rid of it. Just ... hide it. Will you do that for me?'

Gunnar mumbled assent and went back to sleep.

The horses tossed their muzzles, their manes ruffled by the north wind. Thyri calmed them with soft words as the journey wore away.

# CHAPTER THREE

# **REALWORLD**

Philip says there was something like a WebCrash back in the year 2000.

The Stone Age computers they had back then couldn't cope with the year numbers changing from 19 hundred to 20 hundred and it's going to happen again at the Digital Millennium – the year 2048 – because if you write out 2047 in base two (the number systems computers use) you get 11111111111 – eleven spaces full of ones. But 2048 is 100000000000 – *twelve* spaces, mostly zeroes.

But there was nothing special about the WebCrash date, January 4, 2028.

I peeled off my Websuit – as you know, it's like getting out of a wet suit – and padded to my bedroom.

At first everything seemed normal. Glancing through the window I saw it was a bright winter's day. The town's OzoneHole dome sparkled against the blue of the sky, even obliterating some of the Tennessee Fried Ostrich laser ads painted on the clouds.

I ordered an isotonic soda from my RoomChef – it's always good to replace your body fluids after a session in the Web – but a cappuccino coffee came spurting out of the little hole in the wall. That wouldn't have been so bad, but it emerged backwards: chocolate first, then cream, then coffee, and no hot water. After watching the RoomChef's little robot arms trying to froth up a coffee that didn't exist, I gave up.

I didn't think too much of it. If you live in the sort of

home where nothing *ever* breaks down then you clearly don't have a kid brother like that little egg George, who *fiddles* with things.

With a sigh of resignation, I flopped down on my bed. 'Wall, on.'

The bedroom wall chimed softly, sort of fizzed, and stayed blank.

'Wall—'

'Good evening, Sarah,' said the bedroom.

Evening? It wasn't yet 10 a.m.

The bedroom gets its time from the Global Clock, which works from a satellite in high Earth orbit, and I knew that was one gadget that even George couldn't mess up. It was only then I had the first prickling of unease. Something was *seriously* wrong.

'Wall, *on*!'

It took fifteen minutes of trying before I managed to tune into any of the 168 channels the wall normally provides. And when I did, all there was to watch was news.

The world, it seemed, had gone *crazy*.

In London there had been a car crash – the first in five years! – there were pictures of the drivers, unhurt, scratching their heads and looking in bewilderment at the dents in their SmartCar bumpers. The News Robot said the Global Positioning System (GPS) satellites had all gone offline and all the SmartCars were losing their way, and I could well imagine what a disaster that would prove to be, because I know people who can't find their way to the *bathroom* without their GPS wristwatches.

Right across the country the superconductor power grid was shorting out. Not only that, it wasn't being fed enough power from the orbiting PowerSats.

And the microwave beam from one of the Sats, which should have been focused on a field of receptors in the Orkneys, had strayed across Scotland. An aeroplane crossed its path. Luckily, it was unmanned but its cargo of pizzas arrived in Glasgow well-cooked.

In Parliament, the Robot Speaker – screaming 'Order, order!' – had attacked the Leader of the Opposition with its gavel. Of course that isn't too serious. It took twelve members of parliament to wrestle it to the ground.

Manchester–Newcastle were playing an exhibition football game against a team of clones from China – nothing unusual about that – but the manager, IBM's Deep Blue 27 computer, was having some trouble. The players' implants seemed to be going wrong and half the team were playing towards their own goal.

And so on!

The same kind of news was coming in from around the world. What news there was, as half the Combats had gone down too.

In the US, the weather control system in Kansas had gone wrong and tornadoes were scouring across the plains, like scenes from *The Wizard of Oz*.

In Russia, the EarthCore mining project had gone off track. The Mole had emerged in the middle of Moscow, hundreds of kilometres off course, and huge fountains of lava were gushing out of the heart of the city.

In Japan, the city of New Tokyo – where all the buildings are Smart, are controlled by computer and change shape every day – had shut itself off. New Tokyo literally fell down overnight. There were pictures of people standing around amid heaps of plastic walls, or stuck inside Smart furniture that suddenly wouldn't let them go.

And on, and on. Some of it was trivial, even funny. Some was a lot more serious. Nobody yet understood what was going on.

But the commentary robots were already calling it *WebCrash*.

There was one intriguing bit of news, though: about the SETI programme.

*SETI*: the Search for Extra-Terrestrial Intelligence. Listening for radio signals from aliens on remote planets. That had been going on, in one form or another, since the

1960s. But it was only in the 2020s that anybody put any serious money into it. And it was only earlier last year, 2027, that anything was picked up.

It was just a thin radio whisper, dots and dashes, washing over the Earth from the stars, picked up by sensitive radio-telescopes.

You must remember the excitement. Maybe you entered the big Web competitions to try to decode the signals.

Then early this year, 2028, the trickle of data from the SETI search suddenly became a torrent. It turned out, the commentators said, that the signals had been so powerful that even ordinary radio receivers had been capable of picking them up.

Most computers are pretty dumb. As they hadn't been programmed to recognize alien data they had treated it as nothing more sinister than a BBC robo-gardening pro-gramme. Around the world computers had started storing the data wherever they could: in home systems, in public systems like traffic control …

And even in the Web, I learned now. That's right: *there are alien signals, stored in the Web!* Maybe, I guessed wildly, that was the cause of the WebCrash. And—

And that was when the walls went blank, and the bedroom started blinking again.

Warning messages scrolled over the walls saying that Philip's direct-debit bill payments, normally made once a second from his bank account, had stopped, and unless they resumed, our house would be cut off (except for the essentials, of course: food, heating, TV, milk shakes).

I lay on my bed, stunned. It was as if the whole world had fallen apart.

Maybe if I'd lived through the year 2000 crash I might have expected this. (Philip says he just stayed in bed for three days.) But I'd never thought hard before about how much we rely on computers.

Of course the Web is entirely computer generated. No

computers, no Web. But even in Realworld almost everything we do is regulated by electronic machines: from
the giant brains that run the traffic and the weather
control systems and the power grid, to the tiny machines
too small to see embedded in the walls and furniture of
our homes and schools, even our clothes. Everywhere.
It's as if we are all living inside the dream of some giant
electronic brain.

Well, suddenly that brain was having a nightmare. And it
was obvious to me that nobody knew what to do about it.

I tried to be practical.

I called Philip, my dad. He was at work at the desalination
plant in Tilbury where they turn sea water into drinking
water.

Of course he was panicking. 'Sarah, are you OK? Stay
where you are. Don't touch anything.'

I suppressed a sigh. 'Philip, I'm fine.'

'And don't spin into the Web … Where's George?'

'At the PrimateZone.' The PrimateZone is a jungle gym (a
kid brother zoo). The whole point of the Zone is that the
kids blow off steam by doing physical things – running,
jumping, climbing, fighting, whatever it is kids do. There's
hardly any electronic input as it's supposed to be a balance
for Webtime, when you have to lie pretty much still for
hours on end.

So I knew George would be OK there, and, after a little
more agonizing, Philip agreed.

'I'll come home,' he said.

'How?' I asked reasonably. 'Walk? As far as I can see
everything's down.'

He started some crazed rambling about borrowing a
bicycle, but as, even without the traffic jams, it would have
taken him a good month to make it home on *that* – as I
reasonably pointed out – it wasn't such a good idea.

'The thing to do,' I advised him sternly, 'is to stay put
until all the fuss dies down.'

That was when the line went dead. I could only

hope he'd do what I told him.

Parents. You never know what they are going to get up to next. But in the end, you know, you have to let them take responsibility for their own safety. Still, Philip was a trustworthy sort, and I knew I didn't have to worry.

So, as far as I knew, my family were safe.

That left *me*.

I was safe enough sitting in my bedroom, of course. England is really a pretty stable place. It wasn't as if I was in California, for instance, where the SmartQuake control systems had already gone down. I could just sit and wait for things to get back to normal. I might even be able to persuade the room systems to give me something to eat.

Maybe.

But I was already bored. (If you want to know how bored, you try sitting in a turned-off bedroom for more than fifteen minutes.) And besides—

I was a little scared. Not by the WebCrash itself. Most systems have enough fail-safes so I knew not too many people around the world would come to any harm. No, I was scared by somebody who didn't even exist: Numinus Torca, Regent of the Empire of Galaxias.

You may think that's foolish. Numinus wasn't even real. But you didn't see the look in his eyes.

I knew the rules about Domain Breaches. Even if they occurred there was no way a phace, even one as devious as Numinus, could escape from his home world and reach another. And there was *no* danger he could do any damage in Realworld.

Those were the rules. But this was WebCrash Day, and the rules didn't seem to be working …

I went back to the spare bedroom.

Of course I had no way of knowing if the Web itself was still working, given all the problems elsewhere. And I was about to disobey Philip, which, despite the black propaganda put about by George, is not something I do lightly.

But I had to find out what had happened to Numinus.
So I suited up and spun back in.
*Big* mistake.

# CHAPTER FOUR

# BREACH

I was back on the bridge of *The Empress's Mighty Fist*, and immediately in a lot of trouble.

The ship shuddered, as if rammed from below.

Numinus yelled and stumbled. 'Pilot! Curse you, tell me what's happening!'

I scrambled to get control of the ship, while Numinus yelled in my ear.

What can I tell you about Galaxias?

The basic idea is that in a few centuries from now humans will have developed interstellar travel, so that it takes only a few weeks to travel from star to star.

The scientists set this up and fast-forwarded it for a while (a month or so, but hundreds of years inside the Domain!). And then they let Browsers in to see what had happened.

How will society evolve when it becomes as easy to travel to the stars as to fly around the world?

The scientists imagined that humans of the future, with such terrific technology and power, would use it to do good. On the colonized worlds there would be a wonderful Utopia, a time of peace and plenty. Meanwhile, peaceful exploration ships would push deeper into the Galaxy finding new star systems and perhaps new alien races.

Because the machines could provide everybody with everything they needed – food, clothing, entertainment – there would be no conflict. Nobody even needed to work.

And so there would be no crime, no war, no money. Adults would sing and children would skip about smelling flowers.

*Hah!*

The scientists turned out to be dead wrong, as I could have told them. After all my kid brother George and his bratty friends are given everything they need (by parents who can't see them for the horrors they are). And *they* fight like cats and dogs.

While Galaxias was being fast-forwarded, there was intensive weapons development and a bloody war between the stars. Real science fiction stuff with interstellar battle-cruisers and ray guns, even if it did only take half a day in Realworld time. After which a huge and cruel Empire emerged and took over the colonized Galaxy. It was about as peaceful as a Labour-Liberal party conference.

Maybe you can see why I decided to go there.

It's a tough place, but as Domains go its pretty exciting. With a dozen fully realized planets and hundreds of sketches, it's the most gigantic Domain of all, and you do get to fly around the Galaxy. Not as good as a game zone, but not bad for schoolwork.

Anyhow I got a job of sorts as a Pilot of *The Empress's Mighty Fist*, one of the cute little two-person starships they have (or will have). My assignment was to ferry a Bad Guy across the Galaxy.

The Bad Guy in question was Numinus Torca, and he was the Regent. He used to be the heir to the Plutonium Throne of the Empire itself. All he had to do was wait for his mother to retire, or die of old age, and he would have been Emperor of a thousand worlds.

But he got impatient.

When his mother, the Empress, found out exactly *what* he had been putting into her breakfast cereal to hurry along the succession, she got a little angry, and Numinus had to flee, fast. And he picked me as his getaway driver!

I had to fly our two-person ship out of the Imperial Palace, which is a space station orbiting a giant star, and evade Imperial Trooper fleets, before we reached the security of n-space. (And believe me, that part was a *lot* of fun, but I haven't got time to tell you about it here.) Now I was supposed to be taking Numinus to a planet called Raq where he thought he might find allies to help him start over and build a fleet to attack his mother once more.

You might wonder what I was doing running with such a Bad Guy.

As it happens I was a double agent, in the pay of the Imperial Guard, and I happened to know there was a hefty police force waiting for Numinus on Raq. But that's all rather complicated, and academic anyway because we never got as far as Raq!

The signal of the Beacons flickered, faded like a lighthouse in a storm.

The Beacons were like navigation satellites in n-space. But they worked directly on my mind.

The ship's controls were hooked directly to my brain through the control helmet. The whole ship felt like an extension of my body. Navigating the ship was less like driving a car, say, than walking towards a clean yellow light.

But now n-space gusts crossed the face of the Beacons' beam, and I tried to balance the ship, resisting the battering of the current. It was like walking a tightrope.

'I don't know where we've been pushed by the storm,' I told Numinus. 'But I still have the Beacons. I think I can take us home.'

'Home? You mean Raq?'

I knew it wouldn't be that simple, because bright red warnings about a Domain Breach were still scrolling across my vision.

I imagined Web engineers out in Realworld, struggling to disentangle the Domains without doing too much damage. If the worst came to the worst they might have to reboot the Domains altogether, but Domains are so expensive to

run that would be a last resort. I was likely to be stuck here
for some time.

'I mean,' I said steadily, 'I think I can take us back to
Galaxias. The galaxy's explored quadrant.'

'Then do it, Pilot. Get us out of this.'

The n-space streams became still, suddenly. The ship
calmed. In my mind the Beacons shone like the rays of a
sun.

I stirred in my couch, uneasy. This felt too easy.

'I can feel the ship settle,' Numinus whispered. 'Is it
over?'

I sent my senses probing out through the n-space
environment. 'I don't know. I don't like it.'

The n-space sea was as flat as ... a pond? No. My mind
scratched for the right image.

Think about how a huge ocean wave gathers. There's
always an area of calmness in the water just before it breaks.

'Numinus. Find a safety harness. Power up your skin-
armour.' My fingers flew over touch pads as I tried to batten
the ship down.

'What is it, Metaphor?'

The ship stirred as if sucked towards ... a wave that came
at us out of n-space like the breath of a god.

The wave hit.

*The Mighty Fist* tumbled end-over-end, backwards. My
universe smashed to fragments: Numinus's scream, tearing
metal, howling n-space vortices, pain in my own rattled
body ...

This was the Web. It wasn't supposed to *hurt* like this! But
I was in the middle of a WebCrash. The normal rules didn't
apply.

We were hurled out of n-space like a bolt from a
crossbow.

The ship stabilized. The shock of emerging from the n-
space turmoil was like a punch to the stomach.

I opened my eyes. Through a red mist I saw Numinus

push himself from his safety harness, blood seeping from his mouth. The Regent limped to a control bank and poked cautiously at touch pads, powering up external monitors.

I saw a jumble of ice and dark blue sky.

Numinus grunted in surprise. He swung the monitors' focus around.

We were hovering above a world – a planet that curved beneath its blanket of ice. A sun was low. It was morning, or evening. Light clouds floated high above us. Far ahead of the ship sunlight sparkled on an ice-crusted sea.

It looked like Earth, but there were no city lights, no sparks of satellites, no ships on the sea. It was – I thought even then, right at the start of the whole thing – the way Earth might have looked before modern civilization, say 1000 years ago.

I didn't know how right I was!

'Pilot …' Numinus's voice was full of wonder. 'We're in the atmosphere of a planet. Judging from the sun, the ice, I'd say we were over one of the polar regions. Look at the pole, the odd darkness there.'

It looked like a giant curtain, draped over the glittering white ice cap. It was hard even to look at it.

It was a Domain Breach, a flaw in the fabric of this universe. We must have come through it, and finished up *here*, in another Domain altogether. And the Beacons had gone. It was as if Galaxias had vanished, had never existed at all!

But Numinus was still functioning.

This wasn't supposed to happen.

We had come through a Breach into a different Domain. Numinus should have been shut down. I should have been thrown out of the Web immediately.

But none of that had happened.

At the time I had no idea where we were. I just knew we weren't where we were supposed to be, and the Web safeties weren't working.

I did what you would have done.

I closed my eyes. I pushed my scuttle-button.

I gathered a great sigh of relief, promising myself never to take such a foolish risk again. I opened my eyes, expecting to see the familiar, if dingy, walls of our spare room.

But I was still on *The Empress's Mighty Fist*. The scuttle hadn't worked.

*I was trapped.*

Numinus hadn't noticed any of this. 'Metaphor, where are we? Are we still in Galaxias? Have we been thrown into some unexplored quadrant? I've never heard of a world like this.'

I thought frantically. I would have to find a way out of this situation – perhaps get back through the Breach to the Galaxias Domain – but I had to remember that Numinus was a phace. He wasn't supposed to know what he was, let alone that his world was artificial.

He had to know something, but I'd have to be careful what I said.

'No. You *wouldn't* have heard of this world.'

Numinus frowned. 'So? Where are we? Outside the Galaxy somewhere, or have we crossed time?'

I shook my head. 'I think we've been pushed through ... a partition.'

'A what?'

'A barrier between universes. Numinus, I don't think this is even our reality.'

The Regent's breath was ragged, shallow. 'Can you take us back?'

'I don't know.' I pulled my control helmet closer to my scalp. 'The path back through n-space isn't predictable. It might have closed up already.'

'Then the sooner you find out the better.'

Numinus stared greedily at rushing vistas of ice and sea, and I wondered uneasily what he was thinking.

And planning.

# CHAPTER FIVE

# EMERGENCE

In Norrland, Thyri was aware of the Domain Breach, and our arrival. To her, the Breach was a disturbance in the world – a booming from the north, like a distant storm.

When the noise rumbled over her, Thyri's eyes snapped open to darkness. She sat bolt upright. On the other side of the room she heard Gunnar's calm breathing. Light flickered through the doorframe's leather curtains. There was a ...

*WHOOSH!*

... somewhere overhead, as if a great bird had flown past.

(It was, of course, *The Empress's Mighty Fist*.)

Thyri kept a blade strapped to her calf. Among the *karlar*, the free men of Ragnar, there were a few who were prepared to take advantage of Gunnar's blindness and his wife's supposed weakness, to steal their property. She touched her weapon and climbed silently from her pallet.

The air outside the house was bitterly cold. She could see the other buildings – the smithy, the barn, the small bathhouse – a few paces away. The house sat at the summit of a low hill. Around the hill a pine forest lapped like a sea of darkness, utterly still. To the east there was already blue in the sky. The sparse light picked out the hulking mounds that were their metalworking supplies – metal ore, coal, saltpetre – all covered by greased cloth.

There was nobody here.

Another rumble, fainter than the first. Perhaps an echo from the fjord.

She raised her eyes. A thin line of cloud or smoke, unnaturally straight, had been cut across the sky. Slowly the line was dissipating.

'Well, whatever it is,' Thyri murmured to herself, 'it's arrived.'

'Thyri? Is it time to get up?'

'Not yet, husband. Not yet.'

Thyri closed the door and climbed back into her bed. Sleep didn't return.

Meanwhile, somewhere above Thyri's head on *The Mighty Fist*, I was bending over an opened-up control console and watching the repair beetles at work. The tiny golden machines crawled over plastic boards. They nibbled at charred and damaged circuitry, and deposited cubes of yellow silicon like bizarre eggs.

I plucked one beetle between thumb and forefinger. Tiny caterpillar treads whirred on the beetle's underside. Within miniature jaws I saw the blue flash of a laser. It was a neat little gadget. I put it back.

Hours had passed in this new Domain, but just minutes of my Realworld time.

I still couldn't scuttle out, but I could pretend to sleep. While he was fast-forwarded with the rest of the Domain, Numinus just saw an image of my sleeping self.

For me, it was like jumping forward in time, to skip the dull bits.

It had made me a little more scared, though.

Fast-forwarding is only allowed if there is nobody in a Domain (or if everybody's pretending to be asleep, or is somewhere they can't be seen by the phaces). So I knew now that I was almost certainly alone. There was no other Realworld person in here with me.

There was nobody who could help me. And I was still stuck.

The floor slid beneath me. I stumbled slightly.

Numinus was sitting in my flight couch. It was too small

for him. He looked like an adult in a child's chair. He was inexpertly piloting the ship through this strange planet's atmosphere. He caught my glance and stared back.

'The repair's almost complete,' I said. 'Another six or seven hours and we can return home – if the passage is still open.'

The Regent nodded and returned to his scrutiny of the external monitors.

I turned to look.

We were flying low over an island country now, a ring of rock in the ocean enclosing a broad lagoon. At a break in the ring a city sprawled around a harbour. People ran like ants. Sails on handsome wooden craft billowed in the wind of their passing.

Eyes glittering, Numinus took the ship almost to ground level. I saw upturned faces flickering past, a blur of chiselled features. People were diving for shelter.

Then we were over the sea, heading north.

'Why did you do that?' I asked. 'You frightened them for no reason.'

The Regent studied me, and ignored the question. 'Pilot, we may be in an alternate reality – but some of the inhabitants of this place look pretty close to human.' (Did I mention there were alien races in Galaxias?) The Regent tugged at his beard, scheming.

'Numinus, this is irrelevant. We ought to return to the Breach.'

'The what?'

'The darkness at the pole. As soon as the repairs are complete we have to try the reverse crossing. We can't know how long the passage will remain stable.'

Numinus frowned. 'Pilot, with a sub-orbital hop we could reach the pole in minutes from anywhere on the planet. There's no rush.' His fingers rattled on the skin-armour covering his legs. '*Look* at this world, Metaphor. Technologically these people are nowhere. They must be two thousand years behind us.'

'All the more reason not to interfere with them,' I said. But he ignored me.

'We've seen soldiers, but all they have is foil armour and metal sticks they poke into each other. I bet the armament contained in this two-man ship could defeat the combined armies of the whole planet. A man could live like a king here. A man with power ...' There was a light in Numinus's eyes. Muscles worked in his cheeks.

I took a step back. He frightened me. 'What are you saying, Numinus?'

Numinus glanced at me, black eyes glittering. 'Come on. Think. We're a long way from home. The Empire doesn't even exist on this level of reality. What we do here doesn't matter to anybody.'

'Except to the people here.'

Numinus laughed harshly. 'How many plasma cannon do they have? How many defence lasers?' The Regent's tone became sly, almost a whisper. 'We can do what we want here, Metaphor, for a few days anyway. There's not a thing anybody can do to stop us. Think about it. Wealth – all the power you want.' His greedy eyes were fixed on my face.

'Get out of my couch.' I realized now I had to stop him. Not just because of his cruelty, but because I didn't know what damage he might do if he interfered in a Domain he didn't belong to.

But how?

I clenched my fists. They felt small and useless ... but there was a clutch of repair beetles in one palm.

Numinus's expression grew hard. 'What's the matter, Pilot? Don't you like money?'

I tried to keep my voice level. 'What I don't like is the idea of using our power to exploit these people. Numinus, we're not all cut out to be Emperor.'

Numinus snorted. 'We're wasting time. I'm taking her down. We'll land in the middle of one of those coastal towns.'

I pushed the repair beetles into Numinus's face. It was a horrible thing to do, but I didn't know what else to try!

I stumbled back, panting. It was the first time in my life I'd attacked another human being – real or not.

Numinus roared and staggered to his feet. A beetle crawled towards his left eye socket, chewing flesh. It left cubes of silicon in little bloody craters.

It was horrible. But it got him out of my control couch.

I slid past Numinus into my couch. The control helmet nestled to my head like a bird over an egg, and the control systems started reading my brain waves. Smoothly, the ship lifted out of the atmosphere. Stars glittered above an arc of blue planet.

Numinus ripped the beetle off and threw it to the floor. He smashed it beneath one booted heel. Blood ran down his cheek.

He stepped up to me and clinically drove his fist into my stomach.

It *hurt!*

I felt myself double over in the couch, arms folding over my belly. Why, why hadn't I activated my skin-armour? (Galaxias is a rough place – *everybody* wears skin-armour.)

And why hadn't the Web protected me? (I know – it was WebCrash Day.)

My pain flooded into the ship's control system. The ship bucked and rolled. Stars whirled past the view screens.

Numinus snatched the control helmet from me and fitted it over his own scalp.

The ship plunged back into the atmosphere with a kind of wail. Metal tore from the hull and splashed past the view screens.

Clinging to my couch, I forced out words through gasps of pain. 'Numinus … When you hit me I flooded the system … It was the shock … Give me the helmet. I have to get her under control.'

The Regent's palm forced me back into my couch. He was much stronger than me and there was nothing I could do.

I tried the scuttle-button again. Nothing. I was still trapped, with a murderous nut, in a spaceship that was about to crash on an unknown world.

It really was turning out to be one of those days.

We rolled as we fell. Sky and brown land flickered. Detail exploded, mountains and rivers and trees and ...

# CHAPTER SIX

# THYRI

As we fell from the sky, it was mornng in WebVin.

Thyri had gone to Helgo, the main trading centre to the south of Norrland, to buy supplies.

The freighter from Riga bobbed in the waters of Helgo's harbour. Thyri picked her way through the gloomy hold, sniffing suspiciously at cloth-wrapped kegs.

Riga was a Russian port. It was the end of the trade routes that stretched eastward into Russia, the source of furs, wax and honey, and even as far as China which provided silver and minerals like saltpetre.

Like his ship, the Russian trader Caspar was fat and round. He bustled after Thyri plucking nervously at his waistcoat of shabby fur. 'Nothing but the best, as usual, my Viking friend,' he jabbered. 'From the fabled land of China, the finest saltpetre for those renowned kilns of yours—'

'Damp,' Thyri growled.

'I beg your pardon?'

Thyri hoisted a cask beneath one arm and ripped away its surrounding sacking. 'Damp, Caspar. Look at this sacking. Half-rotten with it.'

The Russian smoothed back greased hair. 'Ah. I can explain. We suffered a minor accident, a storm that—'

A bass rumble flapped past Thyri's ears like the wing of an invisible bird. (It was, of course, me and Numinus.) She froze, eyes half-closed.

Caspar was saying, 'We shipped a little water, you see, but nothing that need concern—'

The last echo died.

'Did you hear that?'

Caspar swivelled his round head this way and that. 'Not another rat, was it? I'll flay that lazy crew.'

'No.' Thyri ran the sound through her mind. 'It was like thunder.'

The Russian screwed up his face. 'I heard nothing. I'm sorry. But then, your ears are sharper than mine.' Caspar dried up. His swarthy fingers wriggled together and he laughed uneasily. 'Well, shall we close this deal? Of course I offer the usual discount rates. Find a cheaper vendor anywhere and I will refund the difference, gladly. And naturally you have my guarantee that in the unlikely circumstance of any slight dampness corrupting this fine saltpetre ...'

Thyri let the merchant babble on, hardly hearing.

She closed the deal and hurried home.


*Thyri:* I would come to know her better than I know many people in Realworld.

This was WebVin: a recreation of old Viking settlements, part of a wider Domain that reproduced the Earth of the tenth century. Norrland was a reconstruction of eastern Sweden, the coast of the sea called the Gulf of Bothnia – well above the Arctic Circle, a hard and unforgiving country.

Gunnar had served in Constantinople (the city we call Istanbul today). Constantinople was the capital of Byzantium, the eastern half of the old Roman Empire that had collapsed in the west centuries before. Gunnar had been a member of the Varangian Guard, the elite unit of mercenary Viking soldiers that protected the Emperor of Byzantium himself. He had worked long and hard, saving his money for his wife, Thyri, who waited for him in Norrland.

Gunnar had been a hard fighter, an expensive mercenary, but incautious. At last, trying to defend the Key – a strange artefact he bought from a traveller from the far east – he picked one fight too many. He was left blinded, and all but crippled by wounds to his stomach, back and legs.

Somehow he had made it home, to the Norrland town of Ragnar. And Thyri had had to find strength she didn't know she possessed to reconstruct their lives.

They began to make a living as manufacturers of fine weapons. The expertise and some of the strength was Gunnar's. The determination was all Thyri's.

With time Thyri had grown in stature in the little community. This was not a society where women were given equal rights. But through her courage and strength Thyri came to be considered the equal of any of the *karlar*, the free men of the town.

Thyri had grown stout and grey, her life revolving around Gunnar. He had never given up the Key, the strange little object that had ruined his life. Thyri hated and feared it, though she never understood why.

Gunnar and Thyri had lived long, complex, interesting lives.

Those lives weren't real, of course. Thyri was a Web phace, and her years had mostly been fast-forwarded, crammed into hours or days of Realworld time. But they were real to Thyri, as real as your memory is to you.

Gunnar and Thyri *thought* they were real. And they became real enough to me – real enough to care about, a great deal.

When she got home, Thyri unlocked the heavy chest Gunnar kept in a corner of the house. She rummaged until she found Gunnar's axe. It was the weapon of a Varangian Guard. The blade was tarnished with age but the edge was as keen as ever.

She polished the metal until it gleamed, relishing the feeling of wood and iron in her hands.

Gunnar was smiling in his sleep.

# CHAPTER SEVEN

# CRASH

*The Empress's Mighty Fist* crashed spectacularly, thousands of miles from Norrland. We came down in a desert. And it didn't take long before we were found.

The camel shifted under Efer. The young Arab was dimly aware that the afternoon sun was parching dry the gums of his open mouth. But still he sat and stared.

Two silver bubbles sat on the desert sand.

The bubbles were each twice as tall as a man. They were at the centre of a bowl in the desert a hundred paces across. The sand in that crater sparkled like the jewels of the sheikh, and it was strewn with steaming bits of metal, crumpled as if by the fist of a giant.

A scar in the desert ran from the western horizon all the way to the crater.

There were ghosts in the bubbles.

Two of the shapes looked like people, floating upside-down like fledglings in strange eggs. In the other bubble there were devices, combinations of boxes and discs.

Heat rose from the crater, scouring Efer's cheeks. But his curiosity was strong. He couldn't back away.

The stasis bubbles flicked off.

Stasis fields are like seat belts for Galaxias spaceships. Time doesn't exist inside a stasis field, and during the crash I had been frozen in place, free from harm while the Domain was fast-forwarded around me.

So I missed the last of the crash. It was as if my struggle with Numinus was bad-edited into the now.

I hoped, wildly, that somehow I had managed to scuttle out of this mess.

But I found himself hanging upside-down, staring at the sky of burning blue.

I tumbled a metre or so to a hot surface that crackled beneath me. I heard a grunt as the Regent followed. Bits of bridge equipment rained around us. Repair beetles crawled about, confused.

I stared dimly at my control helmet. It was neatly sliced in half. Obviously the helmet hadn't been totally contained within the bridge's emergency stasis field, and I was glad my head hadn't still been in it.

I dropped my hands to the ground. It was sand, in some patches fused to glass by the heat of the impact. I pushed unsteadily to my feet.

I was in a crater littered with scraps of metal. A scar arrowing west across a desert showed me how the ship had come down, scraping over the sand.

A second stasis field had saved the contents of the ship's hold. A few metres away there was a pile of equipment, jumbled unceremoniously on the sand. So we wouldn't be totally without resources.

We were lucky not to have come down in the sea, I reflected. The stasis fields would have stayed on automatically. We would have drifted to the sea bottom, our static existence noted only by a few incurious fish.

On a normal day, Web safeguards would have got me out of there. But this was WebCrash Day, and *nothing* was normal!

'Pilot.' Numinus brushed grains of sand from his skin armour. Blood leaked from his beetle-chewed cheek. 'Are you hurt?'

'No. I don't think so.'

'Have you noticed our visitor?'

I squinted around. The low, strong light poured into my eyes, making tears stream down my face.

Halfway to the horizon, silhouetted against the sun, there was an animal like – what? It had four legs, a fleshy hump on its back and an imperious gaze.

The beast spat a huge mound of greasy phlegm onto the sand. The Regent laughed.

It was a camel. And on its back was a man swathed in white cloth.

No, it was just a boy. Dark brown skin, black eyes. Long teeth glinting in an open mouth. We were evidently somewhere in Arabia, in this medieval copy of Earth.

Without any fuss the Regent raised his right hand and pointed the centre finger at the boy. A large ring above the knuckle whirred.

A jet of fire lashed at the boy.

The camel reared, crying out in a bizarre, broken voice. Its rider clung desperately to its hairy flanks. The creature turned and galloped clumsily into the distance.

'Numinus, why? That was only a boy. He was no threat to us.'

Numinus blew a wisp of smoke from his tiny gun. 'Missed,' he murmured. 'These ring-weapons are useful, though, aren't they?'

'Maybe we could have spoken to him.'

Numinus swivelled an impassive face towards me. 'And why in the name of the Plutonium Throne should I wish to do that?'

'Maybe you didn't notice, Numinus. But we just crashed.' I bent down. I was stiff, and I wondered if that was as much the first stages of Websickness as due to the crash. I picked up a lump of metal. 'This was once a starship. Now, it is so many bits of slag. Numinus, we are stranded here. And unless we want to camp in this forsaken crater forever we are going to have to find a way to live with the inhabitants of this world.'

Numinus's breath whistled through his nostrils. 'I will

accept I am stranded on this planet on the day I die here. Not before. Come on. Let's see what we've got.' He strode purposefully towards the pile of equipment.

I stared at the empty, level sands. The sun touched the horizon. The sky began to drain of light and unfamiliar stars twinkled at the zenith.

My scuttle-button still wouldn't work, no matter how hard I pushed it. I was stuck here.

I sighed and turned to follow Numinus.

And, out of my sight ...

Efer crawled over the dune's darkened flank. Cautiously, he peeked over the crest.

The two strangers had hung torches above their bowl in the sand. The torches made a puddle of light in the desert night. The strangers – a short, pale girl and the fat one who had unleashed fire at him – walked around their machines, pushing buttons and rapping at panels. Words in an unknown language floated across the sand.

The strangers were making no attempt to hide their treasures.

There was a hot, spiced breath at Efer's ear. A firm hand slapped his shoulder.

Efer's cheeks burned at this silent praise for his find – praise from the sheikh himself.

Silent, dark against dark, the Arab scouting party withdrew into the night.

In the debris from the bridge I found an intact food dispenser, a cube about the size of my fist. I sat beneath a light globe and teased out strips of bland food substitute. I couldn't eat it, of course, and I wasn't even hungry, thanks to my gathering Websickness. But I didn't want Numinus to become suspicious.

I'd set the globe to cast a tent-like cone of light. I'd also programmed in some warmth.

Outside the comforting cone the desert was a sheet of darkness. Frost glistened on the sand.

I shivered.

Numinus walked slowly into the cone of light, scratching notes onto a word pad. Under one arm he carried an egg-shaped instrument I didn't recognize. He lay down wearily and accepted some of my food.

'Well?' I asked. 'What have we got?'

Numinus chewed without relish. 'Not much. Less that works.' He ticked items off on his fingers. 'A couple of Translators …'

Translator machines would also work as communicators. 'What range?'

Numinus shrugged. 'How should I know? It's your ship. They're backpack-sized.'

'They'll talk to a ship in low orbit.'

'Well, that's handy, as there *is* no ship in low orbit. We've got two jet bikes. A digging machine—'

'A Miner?' I said.

'Yes. Various light tools. A couple of intact food and water dispensers. A few dozen repair beetles. And that's about it.'

I took a heavy breath. 'We won't starve, and we can travel.' All I needed to do was to keep Numinus busy until the Web recovered and I could scuttle out. Or Philip came home and used the manual override on my Websuit and got me out that way. 'So where do we go?'

Numinus rolled, picked up the egg-shaped device and tossed it to me. 'Well, I might just have an idea about that. Take a look.'

I studied the machine. Embedded in its smooth surface was a map, a patchwork of green, brown, and blue. Near one edge a single red spot glowed like a fallen star. Now I knew what the gadget was. 'Ah. This is the energy scanner from the bridge. I didn't recognize it away from its mounting …' My voice tailed off. 'And it's showing the presence of an energy source.'

Numinus smiled. 'The source looks small, localized. Somewhere to the north.'

'A single fragment of high technology,' I said, baffled. High technology in Galaxias surpassed anything available in the 21$^{st}$ century Realworld. This was like finding a CD recorder in a bed of dinosaur bones. 'But what a mystery. How did that get here?'

Numinus waved a dismissive hand. 'Maybe it's a relic from a previous castaway.'

I shook my head. 'No. The interface we crossed from our universe is a one-off. It couldn't happen twice.' I was almost sure that was true. Domain Breaches are supposed to be impossible. At the very least they are rare.

'Another universe, then. A third, parallel to both ours and this one.'

'Or,' I said, getting curious, 'suppose it's an artefact from this world's past. A relic of a vanished civilization?' It was a romantic thought. (Completely wrong, of course!)

Numinus chopped his hand into the sand. 'Pilot, who cares? What we have to do is find this thing, see if we can use it. And maybe it will lead us to more such pieces of technology, out of range of the scanner.'

I nodded slowly. 'Perhaps even ... a ship?'

'Or materials we can use to construct one. Pilot, this might be our way off this cursed planet.'

'What's the urgency, Numinus? You were the one who wanted to land here in the first place.'

'For a diversion,' said Numinus coldly. 'Not for the rest of my life.'

'If it wasn't for your greed we wouldn't—'

'Metaphor. Shut up.' Numinus closed his eyes and rolled away from me.

I wrapped my arms around my chest and waited for a chance to fast-forward to morning.

# CHAPTER EIGHT

# EFER

The first touch of sun flashed the frost into steam. Within minutes of dawn a heat haze was rising from our crater. It hadn't been a full night – the Web had fast-forwarded me through the times when either I or Numinus was asleep – but it felt long enough to me.

I felt shivery and nauseous. *Websickness.* I'd spent far too long inside the Web already.

'I take it you're packed, Pilot.' Numinus pushed his laden jet bike ahead of him. It floated a hand's-breadth above the sand.

'I think so.'

We'd left the equipment we couldn't carry in a single, neat pile. At Numinus's touch a stasis bubble sprang into hazy life around the dump. Numinus walked briskly around the bubble, his heavy cloak flapping over his armour.

Something moved in the corner of my eye. A flutter of white.

The Regent returned, looking satisfied. 'That should be safe enough. This world's cavemen, with their pointed sticks, aren't going to break through Galaxias technology.' He stared at the landscape. 'By the Empress's back teeth, what a bleak place this is.'

White robes. White teeth flashing in sun-darkened faces.

A ring of silent warriors rose from the sand. They surrounded our crash site, their sheet-like garments splashing sunlight. I could see metal gleam in their hands.

I tried to get Numinus's attention. 'Numinus, look!'

'What is it?' Numinus turned. And fell silent as he saw the warriors.

The moment stretched.

We were beings separated by more than time or space, and we stared at each other across a few metres of sand.

'Take it easy,' Numinus murmured. 'They can't hurt us.'

'What do they want?'

The Regent snorted. 'What do you think? Our gold, no doubt. Our weapons. What do savages normally want?'

'They may be dressed crudely,' I snapped. 'Their technology may be primitive. But you can see they aren't savages ... What do we do?'

Numinus Torca grinned. His scarred face looked eager. 'We wait,' he said. 'Just wait. Let them get close enough.'

Efer stood in the circle of warriors, heart bursting with pride. He held his gleaming scimitar in an easy grip, just as his father had taught him.

The sun climbed high. And still the strangers did nothing.

Now the sheikh took one step forward. With a grand flourish he threw down his scimitar and raised his arms. 'Join our caravan. Share our food and milk ...'

And so on. It was a speech of welcome Efer had heard many times before.

The two strangers whispered to each other but did not reply.

Finally the sheikh hauled his weapon from the sand and stepped back into the circle. 'So, they refuse our hospitality.' His eyes rested on Efer. 'Boy? Which is the coward who spat fire at you?'

Efer took a deep breath. 'The fat one!'

The sheikh grinned. 'Then he is yours.' And he stepped forward.

This time the warriors followed. Efer took one step after the rest. Then another. And another, until he was running with the men, screaming and brandishing his blade.

It wasn't real. I *knew* it wasn't real. I kept telling myself that this was just the Web. That I couldn't be hurt here.

But these desert tribesmen, their skin like leather, their teeth like white blades, looked real and threatening enough to me.

'Here they come,' Numinus hissed. 'Hold your ground, Pilot.'

'Numinus, let me unship one of the Translator packs. Maybe we can talk to them.'

'Are you kidding? *Look* at them.'

'That tall one threw down his sword. Maybe it was a sign that he wanted to talk.'

'Is your armour powered up? Pull up your hood. Fix your facemask.' Numinus's right hand worked. Something slipped from his cloak and nestled in his palm.

I got even more frightened. 'What are you going to do?'

Numinus didn't reply.

And then it was too late because the tribesmen were no longer a distant abstraction, like images on a TV wall. They were *here*, mere metres away, running at me with their swinging blades ...

Numinus swung his arm high. Something glittering soared above the warriors.

'Numinus! No—'

Efer barely noticed the sparkling thing in the air. His blood pounded and the blade was a live thing in his hands.

Then it was as if the sun touched the desert.

His eyelids shrivelled and peeled back. And Efer saw no more.

I knew how Galaxias weapons technology worked. But I'd never seen such a thing close up before.

The plasma grenade vaporized those closest to it. It merely killed those a little further out.

Numinus Torca, his cloak scorched away, stalked in ebony armour through the lingering glare. Where a huddled, bloody form still moved, he pointed a deadly ring-weapon.

Tears flooded my eyes, so I couldn't see. You can't smell or taste anything in the Web, and I was glad of that.

*These weren't real people.* I kept repeating that to myself. But it had been real to them. And it had *felt* real to me.

Numinus rejoined me, grinning.

'Numinus.' I was almost in tears. 'You barbarian.'

Numinus assumed an expression of mock innocence and waved beweaponed fingers. 'I've been more than merciful, don't you think?'

'Numinus—'

'Drop it, Pilot.' There was steel in Numinus's voice. 'I did what I had to do. Now let's follow that sensor trace.'

I couldn't see any choice. If I followed him, I might find a way out of here. If not, maybe I'd at least be able to stop him next time.

I promised myself I would look up that phace – the Arab boy – if and when I got out of this, and find out who he was. He couldn't have been any older than me.

I would tell his story – and so I have. But that was for the future.

The desert flew beneath our bikes, and the bloodied crater was soon hidden beyond the horizon.

# CHAPTER NINE

# GUNNAR

The hooves of the two horses clattered over frozen ground. Thyri watched their great heads nod as they made their stolid way along the coast road towards Ragnar.

She had concluded her latest business in Helgo the day before. Now she faced a good half-day's travel home to Ragnar, and she'd set off before dawn.

To her left the mountainous land was a sleeping giant, still wrapped in darkness. The sea moved restlessly to her right. The stars overhead were like an echo of the ground frost.

Thyri felt at peace. Her cart was empty of stock and she had gold in her purse.

She'd struck a good deal with that fierce-looking Varangian mercenary commander. Thanks to long hours listening to Gunnar's war stories, Thyri was able to speak the same language as the soldiers. Thyri smiled, remembering the warm ale they'd downed, the food they'd eaten, and she felt ruefully aware of the growing layer of flesh around her middle.

Things were comfortable. The presence of the short iron sword at her waist seemed almost absurd, as did her vague, almost superstitious fears of the last few days.

Maybe it was time to put the past away. She'd been too withdrawn from Gunnar, too fearful for her husband's safety, perhaps. Well, they could afford to work off a little fat now. They could head up into the forest above the snowline. Gunnar could teach her a few old hunting tricks.

There was a sound behind her. A hissing in the air.

The horses stumbled into each other, whinnying. The cart tipped into a rut. Thyri was flung out, dumped on her back.

Within a second she was on her feet, sword in hand.

Two box-like objects sailed through the dawn air. They made a noise like rushing water. They carried torches that splashed pools of yellow light over the road.

There was a person astride each box, riding like Valkyries!

The Valkyrie boxes rocked over Thyri's head. Her hair whipped up in their breeze. There was a sharp smell, a tang like the sea's. A masked face, blank as an insect's, turned down towards her.

Then the boxes were gone.

Thyri stood there, breathing hard.

The boxes were heading north. Towards Ragnar.

Gunnar was alone there.

The horses stood awkwardly in their tangled harnessing. The cart was intact but stuck. Thyri hauled at it, in vain.

She didn't have time for this.

Her sword of iron slashed through the strips of leather attached to the younger horse. 'I'm sorry about this, girl,' she said as she clambered onto the filly's bare back. 'Now, move!'

The village was a splash of stone in the mouth of the fjord. Hanging in the air, I watched people emerge from their tiny dwellings and point to the sky.

I recognized this place. The last time I saw it, I was in the comfort of a Search Engine. This was WebVin, Viking country. AD 973.

We had flown all the way here from the southern deserts. I'd managed to fast-forward most of it, but still the Websickness was creeping over me – and still my scuttle-button refused to work.

Numinus was studying the energy sensor taped to the

control column of his bike. 'Pilot! How accurate is this thing?'

I shrugged. 'It depends.'

'On what?'

'On the size of the source. On its shielding. On its location. If it's buried, for example, a source might not show up at all.'

'All right.' The Regent pointed. 'That way, I think. A few kilometres along this fjord.'

Some of the villagers were hauling out weapons: spears, javelins, bows. This was the tenth century. There wasn't even gunpowder here.

These people were impossibly brave, I thought. But they had no chance against Numinus and his technology from two thousand years in their future.

I tried to distract Numinus. 'Let's go.' I urged my bike forward. There was no reason for these people to suffer at the hands of the Regent.

Reluctantly, Numinus followed. The villagers and their clumsy weapons were whipped away.

We passed over a scattering of crofts and other dwellings. Numinus slowed his bike to a crawl. 'Here,' he said. 'I think.'

We hovered over a hillock's flat summit. There was a single long building, of cut turf with a thatched roof, and three smaller outbuildings. Smoke reached up from a crudely-cut chimney. A horse grazed in a paddock to the rear of the house. Heaps of supplies – ore and fuel perhaps, covered in cloth – were scattered around the buildings. There were no people to be seen.

We drifted to land a few metres from the house. I climbed stiffly from my bike and unfixed my face mask. The unfiltered air was cool. I imagined the scent of wood smoke and the ozone taint of the bike drive, but this was the Web, and I could smell nothing.

I felt dizzy. Websick. I knew I would have to be careful how I moved.

'Pilot. Come and explain what this cursed sensor's telling me.'

The sensor showed the energy source as a fuzzy disc which overlaid a map of the area. The map included a schematic of the house.

'Well?' he demanded.

'This thing can't give us a more accurate fix, Numinus. We are seeking a small, low-output device that is shielded somehow. Maybe buried.'

Numinus tapped the sensor with one ringed finger. 'So what do we do?'

'You climb off your bike and we search. I suggest we start there.' I pointed at the house. 'And, Numinus. This time let me take a Translator. We need information more than we need corpses.'

Numinus unpeeled his armour hood and gloves. 'All right, Metaphor. Lead the way.'

I took a Translator from one of my bike's panniers. It was backpack-sized with an independent anti-gravity unit, so it floated a metre or so off the ground. I shoved it ahead of me towards the main house.

The door was a massive wooden slab. It would not open to Numinus's shove. I walked around the little building. There was a single window cut into the wood, unglazed. A leather sheet was fixed across the cavity.

The leather twitched minutely.

I rejoined Numinus. 'I think there's someone in there.'

Numinus grinned. 'You don't say.' He raised one arm-oured leg to the door. Skin-armour servo-motors whirred as Numinus's boot flew at the wood.

There was a splintering crunch.

The Regent cleared the door frame of debris, then led the way into the gloomy interior. I followed, shoving the Translator box ahead of me.

We stood in darkness. With an impatient snort Numinus threw a small light globe to the ceiling.

Dazzled, I saw two straw pallets, benches along the walls,

a crude table piled with bowls and plates, a fireplace, a few chests and boxes.

And, standing in front of us, a giant of a man.

He was wearing a shirt and breeches, with a tunic over the top. The tunic was brightly coloured, with braid edging. He had a silver pendant around his neck, a big silver hammer. He had a beard, neatly trimmed, and a conical helmet made of metal – iron, probably – with a big nose-guard, and holes for his eyes.

He held up an iron sword. *He was a Viking warrior* – the most terrifying sight I had ever seen.

He spoke, and the words were guttural and harsh, beyond my understanding.

I could tell he was threatening us, though.

But, under the helmet his eyes were wrapped in a dirty bandage, and I could see that his free arm dangled at his side, limp.

My fear subsided, but my heart sank. This old man could not pose a threat to Numinus.

Numinus surveyed the battered warrior with a widening grin, like a cat studying a bird.

I wanted to avoid trouble. I stepped forward, arms spread out. 'It's all right. We won't hurt you. We only want to talk.'

Numinus laughed. 'You're wasting your time, Pilot.'

I kept talking, but the warrior just stood there silently.

'Numinus, this is an old man. He can't harm you.'

'But I can't talk to it until it says enough for the Translator to work on, can I?'

'No. But he's a *he*, not an it.'

'Make it talk,' the Regent snapped. 'I've got questions to ask.'

'Numinus—'

'If you don't I will. Understand?'

I took another step. The warrior raised his sword, and I stopped, waited in silence. Finally, the warrior spat a string of guttural words. I thought I could hear echoes of the languages we learn in school – German, Swedish, even English.

Suddenly, the Translator function cut in. The warrior's voice was edited out of my hearing and replaced by recognizable words. '... who are you to dare to break into the house of Gunnar? I was a Varangian Guard, and I may be old but I learned a thing or two—'

'Your name is Gunnar,' I said.

Gunnar visibly jumped at my comprehensible words. He fell silent.

'At last,' Numinus growled.

I moved cautiously to one of the long benches and sat on hard wood. 'Your name is Gunnar,' I repeated.

The warrior's sightless gaze stayed fixed on my face. 'What if it is?'

'Well, Gunnar, my name is Metaphor. All right?'

'Metaphor.'

'My friend and I have travelled ... a long way. From a country across the sea. You understand that, don't you?'

The warrior nodded hesitantly. 'Are you frightened of me?'

'Yes,' I said.

He opened his mouth – his teeth were terrible, like worn gravestones – and he laughed. 'So you should be.' He paused. 'You're just a girl.'

'Less of the *just*,' I said.

'My eyes scare you, don't they?'

I had to admit they did.

He laughed again. 'Don't worry. The great god Odin is one-eyed. He gave one of his eyes for understanding. I gave both mine, so that must make me the wisest man in the world, ha!'

A lot of complex feelings swirled inside me. Here was this huge, intimidating warrior – a *Viking*, after all – and he was still threatening us. But he had found time to be kind to me.

Sometimes I wish people, real or not, weren't so complicated.

There was nothing complicated about Numinus, though.
He was growling impatiently.

I said to Gunnar, 'Sir, we're looking for something.
Maybe you can help us.'

'I don't know. What is it? Why should I help you? You
break into my house—'

'Well, Gunnar, it's a little hard to explain …'

Numinus and I sat side-by-side on the wooden bench,
listening numbly as Gunnar – who'd quite forgotten we
were intruders – launched into yet another fable about his
exploits with the good old boys of the Varangian Guard.

I said quietly, 'This Gunnar is either a great liar or a fine
warrior. If it's the second, I hope I never get on the wrong
side of him.'

Numinus checked a chronometer. 'We haven't time for
this, Pilot.'

I shrugged. 'Well, you try explaining the concept of an
energy scanner to a battered old man out of the Iron Age.
Let him ramble. We'll get what we want.'

Gunnar was talking about an adventurer he'd once met,
someone who'd been to the far north, where the gods lived.

Numinus murmured to me, 'In my bike I have some …
facilitating equipment.'

I stiffened. 'A MindDump, you mean?'

The Regent's face hardened. 'That's not recognized termi-
nology, Pilot.'

'A Dump is a Dump by any name. You'd use such an
instrument on an old man? Numinus. Listen to what he's
saying.'

'… and so Olaf travelled far into the north, to the land of
the Aurora, and sure enough he found the Sky Longboat. It
was very old, it was built by the gods to fly to Valhalla
hundreds and thousands of years ago, and it was buried in
ice and snow …'

'Pilot,' Numinus hissed, sitting erect. 'This is it. A *Sky Longboat*. What does that sound like to you? It's a ship. If we can fix it ...' His eyes narrowed. 'We can resume my plan. Live as kings on this dunghill for a while, then return home.'

I thought quickly. It wasn't impossible that a craft from Galaxias, or some other Domain, had come here before us. It might have been centuries ago for Gunnar's people, even if it was only a week ago for me.

But there was still something wrong.

'It makes no sense, Numinus. If the ship, if that's what it is, is so far to the north, why did our sensors bring us *here*?'

Gunnar was still talking. '... Well, Olaf came back on foot through all sorts of dangers. And to show where he'd been he brought back something from the northern wastes. *It was a Key to the Sky Longboat*. Well, we got drunk, we fought, we played cards, and he had to give the Key to me. But then a band of Byzantine cut-throats got hold of me, and—'

Numinus jumped from the table, took two long strides and clasped Gunnar's shoulders. 'Old man, this ... Key. It has to be what we're looking for. Now, where is it? Will you give it to me? Eh?' He shook the warrior briefly.

Gunnar stiffened. 'You're hurting me,' he growled. I could hear the threat in his voice, even through the Translator.

'Where is the Key?' Numinus's voice was ominously calm.

'Thyri said to hide it, and not to tell anyone where—'

Numinus punched the old Viking. Gunnar barely flinched.

'Old man. Gunnar. Unless you want to learn true pain, tell me about the Key.'

'No!'

'By the Plutonium Throne!' Exasperated, Numinus stamped out of the house.

The warrior's face was a mask of blood. He was casting

around for his sword, but Numinus had moved it out of reach.

Numinus returned cradling a small black cube. Wires like silver hair floated around the cube. It was, of course, a MindDump, one of the cruellest tools of a cruel Empire. Numinus snapped, 'It really is a stubborn old savage.' He set the MindDump on the floor and began working fine controls.

I whispered, 'Numinus, that brave warrior is more ... alien ... than any creature you've encountered before. He's from an alternate reality! Your device could kill him.'

Numinus ignored me.

The wire filaments stood vertically, quivering as if alive. Then a single filament entered Gunnar's finger, and he jerked as if shocked.

The MindDump was a downloader.

If you download a file from a computer onto a disk, you're making a copy of what's in the computer's memory. The human brain is only a kind of computer, and the MindDump could make a copy of a *human* memory. But it was unproven technology, and brutally destructive.

With horrible speed, the Dump would download the contents of Gunnar's mind into Numinus – and perhaps destroy Gunnar in the process.

# CHAPTER TEN

# MINDDUMP

Thyri spurred the horse, her urgency transmitted through pressing palms and heels. The filly's mouth was flecked with foam.

At last, the final fold of hill fell away. Warned by her instincts, Thyri reined in the horse a hundred paces short of the house.

Suddenly, her worst fears became real.

Her breathing grew deep and the world turned sharp and clear. She felt the muscles of her shoulders harden. Perhaps this was how it felt to be a warrior.

She drew her short sword and her axe. Then she ran to the house, her feet ramming into the earth.

Numinus returned to the house, skin armour soiled. 'Ha! Got it. Just where the old savage told me, in a hole scratched in the soil.'

I was bending over the unconscious warrior, wiping away blood with a scrap of cloth. I kept telling myself this wasn't real, that Gunnar was just a phace, his courage artificial, his pain computer-generated. It was no consolation.

I looked vaguely at the spindle of silvery metal the Regent had dug up, and was brandishing aloft. 'So that's it? Was it worth it, Numinus?'

Numinus toyed with the spindle, tossing it into the air and catching it. 'Pilot, this knick-knack is a Key indeed, the Key that will unlock this fleabag world. And our ticket home. Of course it was worth it.' He strolled to the pallet and studied Gunnar without malice. 'From the old brute's account we'll be able to track down the ancient ship. And wasn't it astonishing, what we found when I dug into its hind brain?' He grinned, perhaps with envy. 'What interesting lives these savages lead.'

'Perhaps we are the savages, Regent.'

There was a noise outside.

I turned my head. Were they footsteps? Perhaps. But it sounded more as if some elemental force were bearing down on us.

'Regent, listen. I think—'

Somebody was standing in the doorframe, sword in hand, silhouetted against the light.

From Thyri's point of view, we were *both* the enemy.

Thyri's gaze snapped around the room.

Gunnar was on the pallet. Blood on his face, clothes. Dead? No, he was still breathing, shallowly.

A primeval growl built in Thyri's throat.

There were two men here – no, one was a girl. She was backing away from the pallet. Thyri saw a slim frame in a suit of shining black, a small, smooth face. (Yes, it was me. This was how Thyri saw my Galaxias avatar!) In one hand the girl held a blood-stained rag. Was the girl hurting Gunnar? No, tending him.

Thyri dismissed the girl as no threat. But the other …

Darker. Fat, almost squat. The face a mask, scarred and bearded. *This one* was the threat. Another black suit bulging with pockets and pouches. Weapons? Nothing in his hands …

Except a silver spindle – Gunnar's Key. She knew that thing was trouble. She should have hurled the trophy into the Gulf of Bothnia.

A shout tore from Thyri's throat, and she threw her axe at the chest of the dark one.

Pale fingers flew over studs on that black suit. The air seemed to sparkle.

The axe hit. The dark one exploded in a glare of light.

Thyri heard a scream. For precious seconds her eyes were filled with light. Then the world reappeared, rimmed in blood-red.

Her axe lay at the feet of the dark one, who grinned at her, and spoke. 'You. Warrior woman. Listen to me. You can't hurt me. I have armour. It is a deflector field. It turns the energy of your weapons, such as they are, into radiation. Light … Do you understand? Well, I suppose it's all magic, as far as you're concerned. You may worship me, at your convenience. And now, if you want this old fool to live I suggest you get away from the door.'

Thyri stood her ground, heart pounding. Think, she told herself. Channel the anger. 'Perhaps your armour will protect your hide, coward. But what about your Valkyrie boxes?' She ran her finger along her sword's edge. 'I saw cracks and joints and pipes. I wonder what my blade would find if thrust inside?'

The girl spoke, her eyes streaming from the flash. 'The bikes. She means the jet bikes. Regent, she could strand us here.'

Thyri smiled. There was fear in that voice. 'So, you are humans, strange as you are. You know fear. Know this. Without your machines you cannot outrun me. And I will destroy you.'

The one called Regent stretched out a finger.

Fire leapt from his hand and cut a hole in the wall. The air filled with the stink of burning wood.

'I could burn you down where you stand,' the Regent growled.

Thyri froze. Consciously, she relaxed her muscles. 'Your threat against an old blind man brings us to a stand-off, then, coward.'

Numinus inclined his head. 'Quite so. Now then, my terms.' He held up the Key. 'I have what I want, right here. And you want the warrior. Let us return to our vehicles and he is yours.'

Thyri nodded carefully. She stepped back through the door.

'Come on, Pilot.' Numinus picked up Gunnar, threw the old man over his shoulder, and walked to the door. The display of strength was startling. But Thyri could hear a whine and whirr, of ropes and pulleys. Some device hidden in his black armour was giving this fat oaf the illusion of strength. Understanding that reduced her fear.

The one called Metaphor stayed close to the Regent, pulling a floating box through the air after her.

Thyri stalked them, trying to close in on them.

The two strangers reached the Valkyrie boxes, their jet bikes. Numinus slid astride his saddle, with Gunnar slumped in his arms.

Something hard slid into Numinus's eyes. Malice. Spite. Thyri saw it. *He was going to kill Gunnar, anyway.*

The girl, Metaphor, saw it too. 'Regent. No. There's no need.' Awkwardly she reached for Gunnar.

And at the same moment Thyri dived at Numinus.

Everything slowed down. Thyri felt as if she were swimming through some thick fluid. Her pulse pounded like a drum.

She wouldn't get there in time.

The girl, Metaphor, was pulling at Numinus's arm. Numinus turned. Rage twisted his face and he held out his hand.

Fire leapt from his fingers and lanced through Metaphor's shoulder, legs. Metaphor crumpled silently. Another flick of that deadly hand and more bright needles shot into Metaphor's bike, turning sections of it to glowing slag.

And then, almost casually, Numinus launched his fire at Gunnar.

As Thyri reached him, Numinus's iron steed flicked into the air. Thyri slammed her fist into its metal flank, making it rock and shudder. But it rose like smoke and was lost in the low clouds.

Thyri stood there, fists working, for one second. Then she

turned and fell to her knees, and lifted Gunnar from the cold ground.

The old warrior writhed, muscles like wood.

'Gunnar. Can you hear me? It's me, Thyri.'

The great grey head turned. 'Thyri. I couldn't protect you. I'm sorry.'

'There's nothing any of us could have done.'

'I have fallen into the snake pit, my love.'

'Just like the first Gunnar.' For Gunnar had been named for a legendary hero who had battled with snakes.

Gunnar jerked, his pain intense.

Thyri's darkest fears settled over her soul, and she held her husband tight.

Afterwards she never knew how long it took him to die.

When it was over Thyri laid the body on the ground. Then she stood and walked calmly to the Pilot.

Metaphor squirmed backwards towards her wrecked machine, pain twisting her face. She left a trail of blood across the grass.

Thyri reached down. Metaphor recoiled. Almost tenderly Thyri picked her up. 'I won't hurt you,' she said.

Metaphor stared at her.

'I want you to live, Valkyrie.' Thyri began to walk back to the house, Metaphor slung casually over her shoulder. 'I saw you care for Gunnar. Perhaps you could not stop what happened. And you fought, at last. Now you will help me again. You will show me how to reach the other. The Regent. And when I find him—'

When I find him, Thyri told herself, then he will fly. Oh, not as he plans, in the Sky Longboat. But as the Vikings have made their enemies fly for generations.

In blood.

# CHAPTER ELEVEN
# RAGNAR

For days, I lay on the pallet that had once been Gunnar's. Days in Web time, anyhow, but as I was out of sight or feigning sleep most of that time it was only an hour or more of Realworld time. But it was enough to deepen my Websickness.

Numinus hadn't been able to hurt me, thankfully. But the Websickness was bringing me down. At least I didn't have to explain my feebleness to Thyri.

And besides the sickness I felt drained, exhausted, distressed by all I'd seen. I kept running it over in my head.

I'd never seen cruelty like Numinus's before, in or out of the Web.

But that wasn't the worst of it. The worst was *doubt*, questions I asked myself. Could I have done anything to stop him?

In the end I gathered my strength. I found I could sit up and even stand, stiffly. Thyri brought me food: vegetables, meat, and a coarse, gritty bread. Of course I couldn't eat – you don't eat anything inside the Web – but I thanked her. I think my refusing food confused her more than anything else.

I had time to watch Thyri, to see something of this Viking Domain in which I'd become entangled.

The Vikings came out of Scandinavia – Norway, Sweden and Denmark – in the north of Europe. Their land was inhospitable, their rulers harsh. And so they sailed the seas, seeking loot and new places to live. In the end they had colonies across half the western world, from the north cape of Norway to France, from Newfoundland in Canada to Russia. They even made it across the Atlantic, and planted a colony in North America that lasted for centuries. And they sailed up the great rivers of Europe, the Dnieper and the Volga, that took them to the Black Sea and the Caspian Sea, where they encountered Byzantium and Islam.

All with nothing more than Iron Age technology, well-made wooden boats, and a lot of guts.

They came to Britain. At one time they controlled half the country, an area known as the Danelaw.

*You* may have Viking blood in your veins. And if you use words like *die, egg,* or *law,* you're using language that comes from the Vikings.

You might think it was romantic to be a Viking. Certainly the landscape was beautiful – the steel-grey ocean, the beautiful dragon-prowed longboats, the firs, and the almost vertical walls of mountains.

But it was harsh.

There were times when I was soaked to the skin and barely able to hear myself speak over the howl of the wind. At least I had decent Galaxias clothing. The natives of the time had only inadequate and smelly clothing, and only a smoky fire and an earth floor or a straw pallet to look forward to at home.

Having lived there, I'm not surprised they travelled far, looking for more pleasant places to live.

Thyri's house was like a long hall. It was made of dry stone and turf, except for some timber walls. There was a living room with a long hearth down the centre, and a small pantry. The other buildings were a barn for the animals, a byre where their food was stored, a smithy, and a bathhouse that was more like a sauna where steam was made by throwing water on hot stones.

The Viking countries were ruled by kings. Our village, Ragnar, had a chief, called a *jarl.* Most of the men were *karlar,* free men, and there were slaves, called *praell.* Women

were discriminated against, I suppose, but it seemed to me
Thyri was accepted as a *karlar*. Certainly she'd have broken
the head of anyone who said she was less.

It all sounds very rigid, but there was some democracy.
There was an assembly that gathered regularly called a
*Thing*, and there was a system of law with a top judge who
would deliver his rulings standing on the *Logberg*, the Law
Rock.

OK, it was far from perfect. But believe me, it was a lot
more democratic than Galaxias which was supposedly two
thousand years more advanced.

And Thyri was kind to me.

That might seem a strange thing to say. After all, I was a
prisoner in her house. And if my scuttle-button had worked
I'd have got out of there as soon as I could. But out of her
warrior gear, she was very different.

When she wasn't travelling, or fighting, she wore a
chemise under a long dress. She generally wore a shawl,
pinned on her chest by a big oval brooch, and an apron.
She had a big belt from which she hung purses, and usually
a knife or two. She wore her hair long but knotted at the
back of her head. Her shoes were skin – calf or goat, I think
– laced around her ankles. She was quite elegant, and kept
herself cleaner than I had expected.

She seemed to have a lot of jewellery – brooches and
necklaces and rings and bracelets and bangles, mostly of
silver – but I learned later that the Vikings had no money,
not even coins. They kept their wealth in silver, but
without coins or banks, they would either hide it in an
underground store or simply wear it as jewellery. They
could always cut it up if they needed loose change.

Thyri had many visitors (she kept me out of sight). Poor
Gunnar had been popular, even if he was past it, and a lot
of people came to offer sympathy. Thyri always welcomed
them with water and a towel, and a meal of bread or meat.

Life was more *civil* than I had expected.

But it was hard.

Thyri spent a *lot* of her time cleaning. There were no domestic robots, no SmartWalls, no washing machines, no dishwashers, no vacuum cleaner, not even running water. And the rest of her time cooking. There was meat and fish – baked in a big oven she heated with hot stones – wheat and oats, cress, even some herbs and spices from overseas, like mustard and horseradish. There was beer, and milk for drinking and to make butter.

Thyri made bread almost every day she was home. She had to grind down her flour with handheld stones, then knead her dough and bake it in long iron pans. It was unleavened, meaning it had no yeast in it, so it was flat. You had to eat it straightaway or it would become too hard.

Of all the things I disliked about my situation, that was the worst, not being able to taste or even smell the delicious-looking bread Thyri baked. But those grinding stones left a lot of grit in the bread, and Thyri – like most of the Vikings – had bad, worn-down teeth.

Oh, and they ate with their fingers. Well, so do I when it's Tennessee Fried Ostrich, and so does my kid brother, all the time, so it almost felt like home!

While Thyri was waiting for me to recover, she would sit down with me and play games when her day's work was done. She had a stack of board games, some of which were like games we play now. Her favourite was called *hnefatafl*, which is a bit like chess. You have to protect your king against attack. (I tried to teach it to George later but the little bug was too dim to understand. Philip liked it, after I'd let him win a couple of games.)

So, Thyri really was kind to me. She tried to look after me, she offered me food, and played games with me. And that was while she was trying to get over the loss of her husband.

Real or not, she was an impressive human being.

My mother died when I was young, so I know how hard it is to lose somebody. I don't think, looking back, I was kind to anybody at the time.

Maybe George, a little.

Thyri had to organize a funeral for Gunnar. He was buried on land, but in a grave that was shaped like a ship, marked with stones. The Vikings believed dying was the start of a journey to Valhalla where the gods live.

Everybody turned out for the funeral, perhaps a hundred men, women, and children. I watched from an unglazed window of Thyri's house. There was a poet called a *skald* who recited, without reading, a long and complicated poem about Gunnar's bravery and valour. It was very difficult to understand, even with the Translator, with lots of comparisons between Gunnar and various gods I'd never heard of.

Gunnar was buried with many of his possessions: his clothes, his weapons, even favourite items like his beer-drinking tankard and his plate. I could see Thyri found it hard giving up all this stuff. I suppose it was as if she was finally letting go of him. But she did it. She kept only one thing. That hammer amulet I'd noticed him wearing around his neck when I first met him. She called it the *mjollnir*, the hammer of Thor. I never saw her without it after that.

I saw all this in fast-forwarded glimpses. Sometimes it felt dishonest. Thyri would come to me and tell me I'd slept for twelve hours – but to me, just a few seconds had passed.

What I'm trying to say is that, for a while, despite the Websickness, despite the fact that everything was fast-forwarded and artificial, I was *happy* there, in Ragnar. Thyri was kind. And although I missed everything I have in my modern world, I quite liked living in such a simple place. It's nice to be able to understand how everything works.

But this interlude didn't last long (a week for Thyri, maybe a half-hour for me).

The Vikings had a code of vengeance. And, gradually, Thyri prepared to take her revenge.

Thyri was working at the house's only table. She spread a

tunic of thick leather over the wood, and used gut thread to sew on scraps of a dull gold metal.

I approached cautiously. 'What are you doing?'

Thyri glanced up and passed me a piece of metal. 'This is mail. Armour. Tough stuff. They say it is imbued with a magical aura. Hallowed by Thor, the Protector.'

I passed back the shard. 'Well, who knows? Maybe there really is magic in your world. Some believe there is in mine. Although if a machine is advanced enough, who can tell if it is magical or not?'

I know that sounds bizarre. By now I was seriously Websick. I hardly knew what I was saying.

Thyri jabbed her iron needle through the leather. 'Mail protected Gunnar when he was a Varangian, although he always complained about how heavy it was. And now, perhaps it will protect me when I go north.'

'North?'

Thyri glared at me. 'We're both going there,' she said. 'Because that's where we'll find your colleague the Regent.'

'But, but I can't travel.' I paced across the earth floor, fingers drumming at the sleeves of my armour. 'You saw Numinus wreck the propulsion unit of my bike. I mean, the part that makes it fly.'

'Then you will travel by longboat and by horse, as I will.'

'A horse? *Me?*'

'I want you with me when I find the Regent. You will tell me things, explain his armour and weapons.'

I sat on the pallet, legs folded under me. 'Thyri. This is not a good idea. The Regent has been trained to survive. He comes from a society thousands of years older than yours. His weapons are sophisticated. You are very brave. And Numinus's crime against Gunnar is … unpardonable, in any universe. But he is strong.'

'Then he will make a fine blood eagle.'

'A what?'

But she would not explain. She simply continued sewing.

# CHAPTER TWELVE

# PURSUIT

The longboat nosed through cracked ice and pushed its way onto the beach.

Thyri and the five Viking crewmen shipped their oars, clambered into freezing water and hauled the boat higher.

I stepped gingerly out of the boat. I staggered a few paces, then dropped to my knees, digging gloved fingers into the sand.

Thyri laughed. 'You told me you sailed from another world. Well, I've never seen a sailor so terrified of water.'

I looked out to sea and shivered. 'And I have never before trusted my life to a thing made of wood and greasy cloth.' It was true. Viking longboats were simply magnificent to look at. The sleek curves of their hulls, their sails and flashing oars, the proud designs of their prows. It was fantastic to think that each of them was handmade. On such ships, protected by no more than leather and wool clothing, Vikings had crossed the Atlantic ocean.

But on a Viking longboat there isn't even anywhere to *shelter*.

During the voyage I'd turned up the heating in my skin-armour and slept as much as I could, trying to fast-forward to the end of this impossible adventure.

A crewman led the first of our expedition's three horses from the longboat. Thyri took the filly's halter and rubbed her nuzzle.

I eyed the animal warily, suspecting the worst was yet to come. I do *not* ride horses, real or otherwise.

Thyri and I left the Viking sailors to make camp under the dragon prow of the longboat. The two of us were going to make our way further north alone. We climbed the back of a wind-blown ridge. A few strands of grass clung to the frozen earth.

There was an oppressive mood of menace.

Under Thyri's prompting, I had to climb onto a horse.

It wasn't as difficult as you might expect. The horse was so huge, patient and solid it was like climbing onto a piece of furniture. I finished up clinging to the mane of my mount, my legs locked to its flanks.

Thyri rode alongside me. She wore her leather armour with its glittering scraps of mail, and she had weapons slung from a belt at her waist. She led the spare horse by its halter. It was loaded with food, water barrels, my Galaxias equipment. The Translator box, with its anti-gravity unit, floated a few metres above the horse, attached by a length of rope.

My Websickness didn't help, of course. But after a while I relaxed, soothed by the steady motion of the animal beneath me. I even gingerly patted the neck of the horse.

Thyri said, 'If I didn't know better, I'd say you were enjoying the ride.'

I smiled. 'I didn't expect it to … to feel like this. This is not a machine. It's another living creature. I'm not used to that. Do you understand?'

Thyri grunted. 'What you mean is the horse knows what he's doing even if you don't.'

'But, Thyri, this is so slow.'

Thyri was looking north. A curtain of blackness hung from sky to ground, looming over the activities around the longboat.

It was the Domain Breach, a hole in the wall of the world.

And this was already a land of dread and fear for the Vikings. I think this Breach must have opened up before, so rich were the myths surrounding this Godforsaken place.

This was a weak place in the fabric of the world, rent open by the WebCrash.

'What desolation,' Thyri said.

'Yes.' I had little to say. To Thyri this must seem a dreadful, supernatural event, and I had no better explanation to give her.

The filly bucked, uneasy. Thyri patted her mane. 'People have survived here before, and I'll survive now. As long as I have to.' She pulled up, staring ahead. She pointed. 'I think we've found your comrade.'

There, on the northern horizon, was an irregular mound of earth.

A few minutes' riding took us to the mound. Thyri dismounted and climbed up the bank of earth. It turned out to be a great ring of broken soil around a pit in the earth, and the pit was the mouth of a tunnel that curved out of sight.

I scrambled up the bank, panting. 'Ah. He's used the Miner.'

'The what?'

'It's a vehicle that travels under the earth. It digs out a tunnel, you see. Its purpose is to dig material from the ground – iron ore, or—'

'He's using it to travel? Why not travel overland?'

I looked into the northern darkness and shivered. 'Numinus is no fool. Why face the unknown dangers represented by the Breach when he can just avoid them by travelling underneath?'

'Well, whatever was in Numinus's mind, he has given us a gift,' Thyri said. 'If this tunnel protects him it will protect us too, and it will lead us straight to him.'

The tunnel was a tube about twenty paces wide. It proved to be straight and regular. Thyri ran her hand over a wall. It was dry to the touch and frozen hard.

'The Miner generates a lot of heat,' I said. 'That must have melted the permafrost, the frozen soil, but it refroze behind the Miner, into a hard surface.'

'Good. We'll make fast progress.'
And so the pursuit began.

The days and nights turned into a clatter of hooves through the frozen darkness of the tunnel.

In my kit there was a light globe. I turned it on and set it to hover. Thyri attached the globe to her horse's saddle with rope. The globe bumped through the air a few metres above her, casting a steady light.

During breaks we spread blankets on the hard earth. Now, in addition to Websickness, I suffered some extremely sore muscles from the endless riding. I slept, fast-forwarding as much as I could.

For days (of Thyri's time) our bubble of light and animal warmth glided through the tube under the earth.

Then, at last, far ahead … there was a light.

Thyri pulled up her horse and dismounted silently. She dragged down the floating light globe. 'Kill this.'

I touched a button. The yellow glow sighed to darkness.

For a few seconds Thyri stood stock still, letting her eyes adjust. The light ahead seemed to unfold. It had a grey lustre, like a pearl.

Thyri bent and, with rapid, confident motions, hobbled the horses with strips of leather. She fixed the Translator rope to my belt.

'Thyri …'

Thyri was a grey silhouette. She grasped my shoulders and stared into my face. 'Little Valkyrie, I know you're not a warrior. And this situation is not of your making. But I need your help. With it I can defeat the Regent. Without it he will destroy us both.'

'But—'

'Now, come.'

Thyri turned and began to pad towards the light. After a few seconds I followed, my breathing ragged. The Translator bumped after us like a dog on a lead.

The going became more difficult. The tunnel twisted

through sharp corners, climbed, and dived. I whispered, 'He must have been quartering the region, searching for the old ship. His energy sensors would not show him the buried artefact until he was close.'

We turned one last corner and stepped into dazzling light.

We stood in a spherical chamber about fifty metres across. A cluster of light globes bumped against the ceiling. On the far side of the chamber another tunnel led away. The Miner sat idle on the chamber floor.

Thyri pulled me back into the shelter of the tunnel. Then she lay on her belly and slid to the tunnel lip for a closer look.

The chamber was still, and silent.

The Miner was a boxy vehicle a couple of metres long. It had huge metal jaws. It was coated in tough-looking blue metal, and windows like eyes squinted back at us. A skirt sheltered wheels which bristled with spikes. Two metal arms held a scarred heat shield ahead of the vehicle. It looked like a mechanical digger's scoop. Below the shield the gleaming jaws hung, idle. Behind the shield an array of cup-like devices craned forward.

I explained it to Thyri. 'See.' I pointed. 'The rock and earth is broken up by ultrasonics from those speakers at the front.'

'The cup things?'

'Yes. They make a high-pitched noise, you see. It's like shattering glass by singing. The shield at the front guards against the heat they generate. Those jaws chew in loosened material and pass it back through the spiked wheels. That nozzle at the back blasts out a hot exhaust. That's what drives the machine forward.'

'No sign of Numinus,' Thyri said. 'Come on.'

Thyri stepped out of the tunnel mouth and slithered to the floor of the chamber. I followed clumsily. Thyri worked her way around the chamber, keeping her back to the wall.

Numinus had hacked crude steps into the earth beneath

the mouth of the second tunnel. Thyri climbed rapidly and peered over the lip. 'It's clear,' she whispered. 'Come on.'

The second tunnel was just a few paces long. It led to another, much larger, chamber. We climbed cautiously out of the tunnel. A dozen light globes cast a shifting pattern of light. In the walls I could see tooth-marks left by Numinus's Miner.

And, resting at the centre of the chamber like a pearl in its shell, was the source of the energy Numinus had sought, the centre of the Vikings' legends: the Sky Longboat itself.

My jaw dropped.

I recognized this Sky Longboat. It was a Search Engine!

# CHAPTER THIRTEEN
# ENGINE

You've seen Search Engines. They are buses you ride between Domains. They're flashy things, designed for effect. They can be any shape.

This one was a spindle shape perhaps a hundred metres long. The graceful midriff was four times as tall as I was. The tips of the spindle were lengthened into needle-fine points.

Its skin, shining like silver, was covered in the slogans of manufacturers and sponsors. Tennessee Fried Ostrich was there and so was the new version of the DreamCastle game zone (DreamCastle II: Dungeon), and ... But all that looked ridiculous, trivial, stuck in that hole in the ground, and with such danger all around!

I remembered now there had been a Search Engine which had crashed recently. It had stopped me surveying more Domains before choosing Galaxias. I wondered if that had been caused by some early WebCrash incident. Search Engines were, of course, supposed to be invisible to the phaces inside Domains, and to make no impression there. This one, crashing, had obviously fallen slap into the reality of WebVin.

I'm not sure how seriously I took Numinus's threats before that moment. He was terrifying. But, I'd reasoned, how much damage can one man do against a whole world, no matter how powerful he is, no matter how crazed?

With a Search Engine, though – and in the middle of the WebCrash – I suspected the answer was *a lot*.

Thyri stepped forward, eyes wide. 'It's ... beautiful,' she whispered. 'I didn't expect this.'

'Yes,' I said, distracted. I was looking for Numinus.

Thyri ran a gloved finger along the hull's grooves. 'Look at this workmanship,' she whispered. 'You know, we sometimes carve runes into the hulls of our ships. To give them power and protection, through the strength of Thor.'

'It isn't quite the same, Thyri.'

I saw something move out of the corner of my eye.

Before I had time to react, Thyri's axe flew.

The blade of the axe clanged against the ship. An object like a small golden nut fell from the hull.

I bent and picked it up. Then laughed. 'Congratulations. You've just defeated a repair beetle. That should slow Numinus down by a few seconds.'

There was a soft sigh. A door had opened in the hull. Maybe Thyri's axe had hit a concealed button.

Thyri grinned and picked up her axe. 'Pilot. Come here.'

The hatch was a circular break in the hull near one needlepoint, about an arm's length wide. A cautious glance through showed us a chamber, small, bare, empty, and closed.

With a beckoning gesture to me, Thyri climbed into the Search Engine. I followed.

I passed my hands over the walls of the chamber. 'Somewhere there must be a sensor that ... Ah.'

A disc of hull metal turned milky and dilated. It was a new door, opening up on the far side of the chamber.

The new door led to a corridor which seemed to run along the spine of the craft. A greenish light filled the air, like the cloudy light of a stagnant pond. To left and right, three doors led off the corridor. And the simple passage ended with a fourth door, straight ahead of us.

All the doors were wide open. There was no sound.

Thyri stepped into the corridor.

Nothing happened. I followed.

The air was warm, slightly humid, utterly still. Thyri

looked at me, shrugged, and crossed in a few paces to the first door off the passage. I followed her. The Translator bumped after me absurdly.

We climbed down a shallow staircase. The room we entered was a disc-shaped slice through the ship. The corridor pierced it like a spine. The walls were crusted with rocks and the dry remains of what looked like seaweed. To one surface clung a cluster of opaque spheres.

'This looks like it was once flooded,' Thyri murmured.

And so it was. This was basically a swimming pool, mocked up to look like the ocean. In here, you could swim around as you surveyed the Domains. An expensive stunt. But it impressed Thyri.

Numinus was not here. Thyri pulled me back to the corridor.

The next chamber was also a cross section of the ship, but the light here was dark brown, mysterious, uneven.

Empty uniforms clung to the walls like fantastic birds. There were tunics bristling with feathers, bones, bits of fur. There were weapons everywhere, like crude guns. And all the uniforms were splashed with what looked like dried blood.

It was paint.

This was a paint-ball room! Probably a crèche, in fact, where you could dump eggs like George and let them flap around firing paint at each other.

'What an oppressive place,' Thyri murmured.

'Yes,' I said solemnly.

'What manner of creatures dwelled here? And what were their gods?'

'Worse than you can possibly imagine, Thyri.'

'Well. Come on, Metaphor. Nothing for us here.'

Once more we moved along the corridor.

Thyri reached the third door. And her eyes grew wide.

It was a room full of wonder. The light was a clear blue, like a summer night sky. Globes like fantastic lanterns were scattered in the air, glowing blue, green, white.

Thyri pushed her face close to a globe. It was slightly larger than her skull, and its light pooled in her eyes. She passed a hand through the globe. Model oceans sparkled over her fingers.

I said, 'Thyri, I think this is a pilot's room, a map room.' Each globe was a different world, probably from a different Domain. One of them must be WebVin. On some of the worlds I could see cities, shining roads.

Thyri walked across the chamber, ducking her head under the corridor tube. 'Pilot. What's this?'

A disc of light lay across the air at a steep angle. Light of all colours swirled through its substance. Around its centre orbited knots of star-like pinpoints.

'Thyri,' I said softly, 'you are honoured. This is your Galaxy. That disc is made up of stars, billions of them. Your sun is just a speckle in that glare.' I hesitated, wondering how much to tell her. 'You are the first of your people to see this sight. And the last, for generations.'

Despite our sense of urgency it was difficult to leave this awesome display. At last, with slow footsteps, we returned to the corridor.

We approached the last door.

Silently Thyri stepped through the circular doorframe.

The walls of this chamber tapered slightly. We must be close to the ship's needle-shaped prow. Greenish pond light washed over two chairs like thrones, tables crusted with glass, walls plated with the black volcanic glass called obsidian. Star fields filled the obsidian panels.

And above one of the tables, hovered Gunnar's Key.

Now I understood what the Key was for. It was a little model of the Search Engine itself. Restored to its proper place, it meant all a pilot would have to do would be to move the Key, and the Engine itself would move in sympathy.

There was a low hum in the air.

Thyri growled. 'That noise. I imagine huge muscles tensing, prepared to hurl this Longboat into the sky.'

I waved her to silence.

A man sat in one of the chairs. He had his back to the entrance. The greenish illumination highlighted black skin-armour. Light danced over a table beneath his hands.

Thyri said softly, 'Regent.'

Numinus whirled, his scarred face contorted.

Thyri's iron sword sang through the air. Numinus's left hand was a blur as it stabbed at panels of his armour.

The sword hit the deflector field in a blaze of light.

Thyri stalked into echoes of brilliance, hands straining for the Regent's throat.

But I got myself in the way. 'Numinus!' I shouted, hands spread wide. 'We've got to talk, to end this!'

Thyri shoved me aside. There was nothing I could do, I was so weak. I crumpled and fell against a bulkhead.

But it was too late. Numinus's eyes glittered with triumph. 'Sorry, warrior woman,' he said softly. A sphere of silver rested in his upturned palm. Another Galaxias weapon.

Thyri took another stride.

Numinus casually dropped the sphere. It shattered.

Something fizzed out of the small explosion and darted like an insect a few metres above the deck, a wavering distortion in the air like heat haze. I was still on the deck, pressed back against a bulkhead. As the fizzing thing passed before me I felt a tugging at my gut.

'Thyri,' I called. 'Stay back. That was a Hawking Shell. It's a tiny black hole, distortion in space. Your armour won't help you if it touches you.'

'How do we get rid of it?' Thyri demanded.

'We don't. And it's unpredictable. It's even out of Numinus's control. It might vanish in a moment, or it might destroy the ship. Regent, you must be desperate to try that.'

Numinus laughed. 'I'm almost ready to launch. I haven't come this far to die at the hands of a crazed aboriginal.'

'And I haven't come so far, star man, to let you live,' Thyri hissed.

'Numinus, it isn't too late,' I said, pleading. 'You are a servant of Galaxias. Leave this world and go home, get on with your life. Forget what's happened here, what you've done.'

An oddly wistful look crossed Numinus's face. 'And what of my … crimes here?'

'Perhaps you can atone.'

Numinus's eyes met Thyri's. The Regent said softly, 'I think there is only one way this woman will have me atone, Pilot. I fear you're wrong. It really is too late.'

For a moment there was a tense silence, broken only by the spitting of the black hole.

I had only one thing left to try. It meant I was breaking all the rules of the Web. But I had no choice!

'Numinus, listen to me.'

The tone of my voice had changed. Both of them turned and looked at me.

'Numinus. *None of this is real*.'

'What?'

'Don't tell me you haven't suspected it. This world is artificial. A model inside a huge computer.'

Thyri growled, trying to understand. 'Like a dream? We are living in a dream?'

'Yes. Something like that. Numinus, the machines are breaking down. That's why your reality – Galaxias – was able to pollute this one, WebVin. *But none of this is real*.'

His face hardened. 'If nothing is real, what does it matter what I do?'

Tough question!

I had no answer. But I had him off balance. I could see that.

Maybe if I'd had a little more time I could have got through to him.

But there was no more time.

The black hole struck.

The fizzing blur shot straight at me. It punched through the centre of my torso!

# CHAPTER FOURTEEN

# ESCAPE

The black hole winked out of existence. But it had done its damage.

If this had happened for real, I'd have been dead!

I stared down at the mess it had made of my stomach. It didn't hurt, of course. But I could feel the Web's modelling programmes kicking in. As far as the Web was concerned I was badly injured. I was going to be restricted from now on, even more than by the Websickness.

Meanwhile, the battle was continuing.

Thyri turned on Numinus with a roar.

The Regent's fingers flew over a tabletop. The nose of the floating Key rose into the air, and the Search Engine lifted in response.

Have you seen that corny old 2-D movie about the *Titanic?* Your parents were probably taken to it as a kid, and blubbed all the way through. (Philip still does when it's shown on Christmas Day.) Remember those scenes where the ship is going down, and the decks tip up, and all the passengers plummet through the windows?

It was like that in the Search Engine.

With my injury I was helpless. I tumbled backwards out of the room.

Thyri tried to leap, but the floor sagged beneath her. She collided with the rear bulkhead. The impact knocked the wind out of her body. Then she rolled after me out through the circular doorway.

The corridor was a near-vertical tube beneath us. I managed to grab the lip of the doorway with one hand. But now the door began to iris shut, like a camera shutter. It felt as if a knife edge was passing beneath my fingertips. For a few seconds I hung there, staring up at Numinus's grinning face. Then I dropped and caromed off the walls to the bottom of the tilted corridor.

I finished up crumpled at the back of the corridor. Thyri fell after me. The Translator box drifted beside us, still attached to its umbilical cable.

The Search Engine shuddered as it tried to rise. I heard its needle nose grind against the roof of its cage of earth.

Thyri cupped my face in her hands. 'Pilot! Tell me what to do. How can I stop him?'

'Thyri. You can't. He's sealed into the bridge.'

Thyri howled rage. She shook me brutally. 'I'll not let him live, Pilot!' I could see she was considering clambering up that tilted corridor, tearing at the bulkhead until her fingers broke and bled.

'Listen to me,' I cried. 'If you stay here during take-off you will surely die. You'll be crushed and choked. Numinus would lie in his couch, laughing.'

She hesitated, and made her decision. 'All right. We've got to get out of here.'

'Yes.'

She grabbed me by my belt and hauled me out through the hatchway into the cavern. The Translator bumped after us.

The skin of the tilted Search Engine shone like the sun. Sparks moved about the advertising panels on the hull. A thrilling singing noise filled the cave.

I clutched at Thyri's bloodied armour 'The Miner.'

'What?'

'The machine. Get us to the Miner. The heat shield might protect us when she lifts.'

Now the Search Engine lifted from the soil. Heat blasted my face, but I was too weak even to walk.

Dragging me, Thyri scrambled through the connecting tunnel into the Miner chamber.

The light here seemed dim as twilight. Thyri ran around the Miner, searching for anything that looked like a door. I tried to focus, but I was weakening fast and couldn't help her.

*There*. An indentation in the hull, just above the wheel skirt. Thyri pressed her palm against the metal. A section of the hull slid upwards and sideways, revealing a small room, two seats side by side. Thyri bundled me into the cabin and clambered after me. With a yank on its rope she hauled in the Translator.

Light pulsed into the chamber. The Miner shuddered. The air roiled.

And the door was still open. 'Metaphor! The door. How?'

My eyes flickered open. 'The red button. To the left of the console.'

Thyri found a red stud. She stabbed at it with one thumb. The door sighed closed.

I found a slit at eye level. I found myself peering at the back of the Miner's heat shield.

There was a second of stillness.

Then a fist of light slammed into the shield.

The Miner was hurled backwards. Thyri braced her arms against the panels before her. I tumbled to the narrow floor. Metal crumpled as the Miner was thrown against the wall of the chamber.

The light faded. Thyri helped me up. I pressed my eyes to the window slit, and saw sky.

The Search Engine had blasted away the roof of its prison. It hovered like a small sun. Dazzling sparks raced over its spindle form.

Then the Engine's nose lifted to the sky – and it leapt.

There was a single flash against the grey sky, a roll like thunder. Then it was gone.

The Arctic night closed over the wound in the earth. Thyri

watched through the eye slit.

I groaned. I wasn't in pain, but I was so *weak*.

'Don't try to move,' Thyri murmured.

'Thyri. Numinus has escaped. Perhaps he will make straight for the Domain Breach, if your world is lucky.'

'No.'

'What?'

'He hasn't escaped. Not as long as I breathe.'

I looked at her. 'Good grief. I believe you're serious. Thyri, do you understand where Numinus has gone? He is at least several hundred kilometres up, moving twenty-five times the speed of sound.'

'You will tell me how I can reach him.'

Gingerly, I touched the blood crusted over my midriff. 'Oh, sure. Here I am, stranded in an alien reality, and I've been punched in the stomach by a black hole ...' I knew I was rambling, but I couldn't help it. 'If this was real I wouldn't even be alive. And now some bone-headed Viking wants me to shoot down a spaceship using nothing but Iron Age technology. Thyri, I miss my father. Have I told you about my father?'

'Yes. Try to sleep now.'

# CHAPTER FIFTEEN

# PLANS

Under my guidance Thyri drove the damaged Miner deeper into the tunnel under the Domain Breach. Then she collapsed the open end of the tunnel, shutting out the disturbing sky of the Breach.

Thyri tried to help me. She rigged up a pallet from Miner seat cushions and laid me gently on it. She placed my Galaxias medical kit on the ground beside me. Silver filaments snaked out of the seamless box and dug into my flesh.

None of this was doing a bit of good, of course. But my injuries were real within the context of WebVin and its inhabitants, and I had to make a show of recovering from them. Once again, I tried to nap so I could fast-forward through hours of recovery.

My real problem, of course, was Websickness.

By now, I estimated, I had been in the Web continuously for five Realworld hours – maybe twice as long as the manufacturers recommend. I was nauseous, dizzy, weak, disoriented. The only good thing was that I was too ill to be hungry!

And all the time I was trying to work out what to do about all this.

I felt responsible, in a way.

Maybe that was wrong. The WebCrash wasn't my fault, and neither was Numinus's passage through the Domain Breach into this innocent world. But maybe there was

something I could have done differently to prevent quite so
many of the people of this world from getting hurt.

But the problems I faced now ... well, think about it.
Numinus was going to use the Search Engine as a spaceship.
Right now it was in orbit around the planet, and Numinus
would be devizing weapons.

If a hostile alien ship was orbiting *our* Earth, perhaps we
could do something about it. We could send it radio signals
to try to communicate with it. We could fire nuclear
missiles at it. We could send up space shuttles and try to
board it. We could even launch an attack from the base on
the Moon.

But this was AD 973!

These people had no radios or rocket ships or missiles.
They had no air travel at all. The fastest way to travel on
land was on horseback. The Vikings didn't even have
*gunpowder*.

And now Thyri, my strong Viking friend, wanted me to
come up with a way to challenge a spaceship!

It was impossible. I shouldn't even have wasted time
thinking about it. Perhaps if I'd been healthy, I'd have
dismissed it altogether.

But lying there with my mixture of real and artificial
sickness, fast-forwarding through time, maybe my mind
was a little looser than usual. I remembered stuff I'd heard
in school about how the Chinese had invented gunpowder
long before the Europeans.

Strange as it seemed, even to me, I started to get an idea
about what we could do about Regent Numinus Torca.

Thyri fixed cushions so that I could sit up. Metal umbilicals
still connected the medical box to my body. 'I'm going to
be a burden, I'm afraid,' I said. 'According to my friendly
box here I'm not capable of walking. My spinal column is
severed. Every few minutes this box flashes lights at me,
insisting that I get to a full-facility Galaxias hospital
without delay.' My voice faltered. 'That's funny, isn't it?'

Of course my injuries weren't real. But my weakness was, and so was my confusion.

'We can't stay here,' Thyri said briskly. 'I have to move you back to Norrland.'

I sighed. 'And we have to take back some equipment, Thyri, if we can. I've been thinking.'

Thyri came close. 'Tell me.'

I toyed with my medical wires. 'I've got an idea, Thyri.'

'A way we can get at Numinus.'

'Yes. We'll need to build something like a longship … a very large ship, strangely shaped. It would be a cylinder, a tube as wide as a man's height, let's say, and perhaps fifty times as long. Do you think your shipwrights could make such a thing?'

'We could use the keel timbers from longboats. But it will be expensive.'

I smiled gently. 'Thyri, we'll take a sensor panel from the Miner. This will show you, for instance, where to find new deposits of tin and iron ore. I would think that could make you rich very quickly.'

Thyri nodded slowly.

I said, 'We'll need to take back all the heavy tools and instruments we can find here. And, most important, we'll need the heat shield from the Miner.'

The shield was a plate of twisted metal that was taller than Thyri. 'Impossible,' she said flatly. 'We could never carry it. We have only three horses, Valkyrie.'

'But my Translator unit has an anti-gravity generator. That's what makes it fly. It can lift anything. Now then, see if you can find a laser cutter among Numinus's tools. It will look like this.'

Thyri strapped the Translator unit to the centre of the heat shield. Then she grappled nervously with the laser cutter, passing its burning light over the shield's supporting arms.

A thread of metal softened, stretched, snapped. Thyri stood back quickly.

The shield toppled grandly away from the Miner and bobbed, rocked, and finally stabilized over the Translator unit, a few centimetres from the ground. The straining Translator whined in complaint.

I clapped my hands. 'It worked! Now I can ride back in style.'

Thyri lifted me onto the centre of the shield, and piled on equipment and Miner parts. The shield bobbed gently like a raft in the air. Thyri fixed ropes to the shield and attached the loose ends to the harnesses of two of the horses. With gentle tugging she encouraged the horses to haul their way into the tunnel.

At first the horses strained, but once the plate was in motion they made rapid progress. Thyri trotted alongside, one hand on the bridle of the lead horse.

'It's like a barge,' I said. 'Once you've generated enough momentum there isn't much resistance. Do you know what momentum is, Thyri?'

'Why don't you tell me?'

And so the kilometres wore away in a fast-forwarded blur.

# CHAPTER SIXTEEN

# DESIGNS

And so it began.

I slept as much as I could. That wasn't difficult given my growing weakness from the Websickness. What passed as an hour for me was more like a month for Thyri. And I saw the construction of what she called the *Mjollnir*, the Hammer of Thor, in fragments and glimpses.

She had little difficulty getting the support of the people of Ragnar for her venture. It must have sounded bizarre to them, but she stood on the *Logberg* and simply showed them the evidence: me, my Galaxias technology, what Numinus had done to me.

The Vikings were explorers. They were imaginative people, ready to accept the strange, and not afraid of huge challenges.

Under my instructions, the Vikings were going to make a rocket.

Within a few days of our return the construction began.

The shipwrights started with the wood. They cut down pine trees and oak trees from the forests, and split them along their lengths to make planks. They also made wooden pegs and wedges, and blocks and supports for the construction of the missile itself. Their main tools were hand-held axes, although they also had knives, chisels and planes. I was amazed how skilful and fast the shipwrights were.

There were iron nails and washers to fix the planks

together. I watched the smiths work with their forges, smelting iron from bog ore. They had bellows, tongs and hammers, and they used shears for snipping off lengths of hot metal. But they had no masks, nothing to protect their faces but cloth tied over their mouths.

One evening, when the construction was at its busiest, I went with Thyri to view the rocket.

Most of the light had leaked away from the dusk sky, but still the teams of boatbuilders, woodsmen, stem-smiths, plank-cutters, and labourers worked on. Lanterns moved through the copse at the foot of the hillock on which Thyri's house was set. Shouted instructions and the pounding of metal against wood floated up to me through the cooling air.

The thing they were building lay on its side in the copse, half-concealed by fir trees. There were wooden hoops that looked like the rib cage of a huge creature, perhaps a whale, stranded there in the forest. A few dozen timbers had been laid in place now and the cylindrical shape of the construction was coming clearer. The hull of my wooden rocket was going to be clinker-built, with the planks overlapping each other, just like a longboat. The shipwrights used wool and pine tar to seal and waterproof the seams between the planks.

I had learned more about shipbuilding than I had thought possible, and it was quite a thrill to see the great craft coming together from my crude sketches. But without the expertize of the Viking boatbuilders it would never have been possible to get so far.

But I spent much of my time fretting over whether it would work at all.

I would sit under a light globe, working through calculations and fine points of the design. I was applying lessons I half-remembered from school, things I'd seen or read in the Web. I longed to be able to get out to Realworld, not just to get over Websickness, but to go to a library and *check* what I was telling Thyri to build. (If you think I was fretting too much, *you* try designing a missile with Iron Age tools!)

Thyri stood over me, eating pork. She had to clear clutter from her pallet before she could sit down.

I noted absently that the woollen blanket on the pallet was filthy and threadbare. The house was barely recognizable as the home it had once been.

Well, I knew that without Gunnar, it was a home no more to Thyri. The house was just another tool. Even the bags of gold stacked in one corner were simply a means to an end. To Thyri now, the rocket – and Numinus – were everything.

'How goes it, Valkyrie?'

'The attitude control is giving me a pain,' I muttered, scribbling. 'This steam-jet system is the best I can dream up ... but you just haven't the technology. The iron pipe samples you brought me simply aren't accurately tooled.'

Thyri stopped listening. I knew she'd long since grown inured to my incomprehensible complaints.

But this was one problem I hadn't been able to overcome – guidance.

You don't just fire off a missile like a Bonfire Night firework. You need attitude control, minor rockets that make it turn this way and that to keep on course. And you need some kind of guidance system, a brain to direct it to its target.

I'd been able to improvize attitude control with steam jets. But I couldn't come up with any way to have the missile guide itself to its target automatically.

When I explained this to Thyri, she had an immediate solution. 'Then I will fly Thor's Hammer myself. I will guide it to the skull of Numinus.'

I tried to talk her out of it. But since I had no better ideas, I didn't succeed very well.

Anyway, my biggest worry was propellant – fuel for my missile. Remember, the Vikings didn't have gunpowder. I had hoped to be able to buy some from China, via Thyri's

Russian trader contacts, but that turned out to be impossible. So I was having to put together a mixture (from memory!) that I thought might work.

'I'm assuming a mix of seventy-five percent potassium nitrate, fifteen percent charcoal, the rest sulphur. I'll be able to pep it up with some of Numinus's grenades to give it the specific impulse we'll need to reach orbit. But we need more potassium nitrate, Thyri.'

Thyri turned her head. 'We need *what*?'

'Saltpetre.'

Thyri nodded, chewing slowly. 'How much?'

She went to Helgo to get it. And that was where, for the first time, we heard about what Numinus was up to. I fast-forwarded to her return, and she told me about it.

Caspar had come up in the world, largely thanks to Thyri's money, the Viking thought wryly. The Russian merchant had bought a fine house on the outskirts of Helgo – no more cheap taverns for him – and he welcomed Thyri with a wave of plump, ring-encrusted fingers.

There was a sofa before a roaring fire. Thyri noted a long blonde hair draped over a cushion. Evidently the Russian was making new friends!

Caspar brought her mead to drink in a cut glass. 'Of course I am delighted to take your new order.' He sat on an embroidered stool, arranged his velvet robe. 'But I fear there may be a little delay. The shipping lanes are somewhat disrupted by the recent incident in the Black Sea.' He sipped his mead.

Thyri felt a sudden chill, as if the wind had turned. 'What incident?'

Caspar's round face showed surprise. 'You haven't heard? Well, it's a great mystery. The Byzantine sages are considering the reports. Some say they saw lights in the sky. I'm rather doubtful about that. What's indisputable is that there was a massive explosion in the sea.' The Russian's small hands fluttered. 'There was a wave like a wall of water.

It hit the coast. The land was scoured away, clean down to bedrock. There had been villages there, small fishing places. Many lives were lost. And who knows how many ships? The Black Sea is still strange. Unusual storms. Choppy seas. And I'm told that those who venture close enough see a crater on the sea bed, glowing red. What do you think of that?'

Thyri said nothing.

'Well, you can imagine what it's done to my schedules.'

Thyri stood abruptly, pulling closed her robe. 'Caspar. Get me that saltpetre.'

'Of course, but—'

'Do it in a week and your fee is doubled. Do you understand?'

Caspar's small mouth fell open. Thyri turned without ceremony and left.

When Thyri got home she told me what the Russian had said.

'It was Numinus,' I whispered.

'What weapon can strike from so far away?'

I shook my head. 'Thyri, where he is, Numinus doesn't need weapons. He's very high up and moving very fast. All he needs to do is throw down a rock.'

'Why attack the sea?'

I shrugged. 'Obviously he has to refine his aim, his range. I suspect he will learn fast. Perhaps the next rock will fall on a city.' I placed a hand on Thyri's arm. 'You see, when your people are crushed, terrified, in turmoil, starving, then he will land like a god and take over.'

'Then it's no longer simply a matter of vengeance,' Thyri said. 'He has to be stopped.'

'Yes.' I smiled. 'But consider this. The longer he dreams in orbit the longer he stays within your grasp.'

'Yes,' said Thyri. 'And my grasp is long.'

'You're very brave, Thyri. You know that if you fly on the *Mjollnir*—'

'I will probably die? I know. But life isn't everything, little Valkyrie. If I die in such a cause – die in removing this scourge Numinus, from my world – then I will be welcomed into Valhalla as one of the *valr*, the honoured dead. And I will be with Gunnar, she regarded me. 'But then, if none of this is real – if *I* am not real – then none of this matters, does it?'

'You are as real as you feel, Thyri. And your courage is real.'

She shrugged. 'Even if this is just a Dream of Midgard-sorm, the world-serpent, then it is up to us to behave as if it were not so.'

'Yes,' I said, but I didn't trust myself to say any more.

Thyri helped me out of the door. I shivered, despite my skin-armour and layers of woollen blankets. My Webtime was up to *seven* hours, I estimated. The battered Translator box bobbled faithfully after us.

Although it was barely dawn it seemed that half the population of Ragnar was swarming over and around the cylinder lying in the copse. Exasperated adults chased children from the attitude control piping and the huge fins.

Over the cylinder stood a scaffolding made of three massive tree trunks. Cables of Galaxias metal snaked over the scaffolding and wrapped themselves around the cylinder. Men tugged at them experimentally.

Thyri manoeuvred the chair down the hill. Children skipped after us, staring at me curiously. I waved weakly.

The workers made last-minute adjustments to the cylinder, pounding in fresh rivets and checking piping. They turned to us and nodded politely, brushing at blond moustaches.

We reached the base of the cylinder. A truncated cone flared out of the base. This was the tail nozzle from the wrecked Miner, and now it was the nozzle for my rocket. Triangular fins reached over our heads, blocking out the light.

'If you're going to succeed,' I said to Thyri, 'it's important that you understand what is going to happen. Now then. This cylinder is packed with gunpowder. You can smell the sulphur—'

'I know that much.'

'I've lumped it into granules of varying sizes. If all goes well the gunpowder won't explode. It will burn steadily for some minutes. Hot gases will make their way out of the nozzle and push the ship into the air. The fins will keep her stable.'

Thyri nodded. 'I understand.'

We walked the length of the cylinder. I admired the workmanship contained in the bands of iron, the polished, caulked timbers. The craft was like some huge piece of furniture.

The other end of the cylinder was wrapped in a nest of piping. I studied the pipes critically. 'Look, Thyri. You will vent steam out of this piping. That will push the ship, direct to its goal. There's a boiler at the top end of the cylinder, just here, powered by a couple of broken-up grenades. Well, it might last long enough.'

We reached the cabin at the tip of the cylinder. It was a cramped, tent-shaped box welded together from the Miner heat shield. It was the best protection I could give Thyri. A seat from the Miner had been fixed to the base of the box which was now tilted vertically.

I imagined being Thyri, climbing into that seat, listening to the roar of the gunpowder. My heart thumped at the thought.

But Thyri showed no fear. This was simply what she had to do.

I peered into the little cabin doubtfully. 'You'll have my-skin armour, of course. That will give you a few minutes' air. Well, it's the best I can do.'

Thyri smiled. 'You're not very reassuring, little Valkyrie.'

The cables connecting the nose of the cylinder to the

scaffolding arced high over our heads. Now the cables went taut, singing in the air.

A foreman came to us, sweat matting the golden hair on his forearms. 'We're ready to lift.'

Thyri nodded. She returned me to the vantage point at the crest of the hillock near her house.

Adults shooed children to safety. Teams of burly Vikings, men and women, spat on their hands and picked up cables. Then, working to low, rhythmic chants, they began to haul.

Cables quivered like guitar strings. Pulleys creaked and rotated. And the metal tip of the cylinder lifted like the head of a waking giant.

Children cheered. The Vikings grinned through sheets of sweat. I whooped too. It was a *fantastic* moment!

Then a cable snapped. The frayed end whipped through the air. It lashed at a scrambling woman, slicing through her leg like a knife through soft butter. She stared at the stump and began to scream.

I could hear the voices of foremen. 'Never mind that. Keep working, you idlers!'

The cylinder rocked. The remaining cables groaned ominously, but they held. Gradually the rocking steadied and the cylinder began to rise once more.

At last, it was vertical. Standing on its fins, wood and iron gleaming, *Mjollnir*, the Hammer of Thor pointed at the sky like an armoured fist.

# CHAPTER SEVENTEEN

# LAUNCH

I had to stay in Thyri's home, following events remotely through my instruments. Later, I was able to reconstruct what really happened.

The cabin was dark, the stink of sulphur overwhelming. The heat of the attitude jet boiler seeped through the floor.

Metaphor's skin-armour was short in the arms and legs, almost unbearably tight around the midriff. Thyri lay in the Miner chair, feeling the armour move over her chest.

Metaphor's voice sounded from the implant in her ear. *'It's time, Thyri. The Search Engine has just risen over the horizon. Close up your face mask.'*

Thyri fixed the mask over her face, sealing its edges with a gloved thumbnail. A plate of glass allowed her to see.

Mounted on sturdy legs before her was a simple instrument panel. There was a series of pads which, Metaphor had patiently explained, would control the attitude thrusters. Half the panel was taken up by a *viewer*, a sheet of glass which now lit up with a panoramic view from the nose of the rocket.

Metaphor asked, *'Is the area clear?'*

Thyri studied the viewer. A ring of people, adults and children, surrounded the cylinder at a safe distance. One man stood near the cylinder, brandishing a torch. 'Yes,' she said.

*'Then this is it, Thyri.'*

'Good!' Thyri slammed her fist into the centre of her

panel. In response, a mouthful of fire spat into the air from the tip of the cylinder.

Seeing Thyri's signal, the man with the torch ran past the huge fins and under the base of the craft. Thyri imagined him hurling his torch onto the bonfire banked there, then turning and running for his life. Soon the first gunpowder granules would hiss and fire.

Smoke wisped. The cylinder shuddered.

'Valkyrie. It's working.'

*'Well, you're committed now, Thyri.'* Metaphor sounded more scared than Thyri. *'You must succeed. Stand by.'*

There was a roar like a bear's.

The cushioned seat slammed into her back. The bones of her skull rattled together. Invisible fingers seemed to be hauling back her cheeks. Darkness framed her vision.

The ground fell away.

Barely able to walk, I stumbled to the unglazed window of Thyri's house.

White smoke was billowing over the ground, huge clouds that towered and flowed up the hillside.

And out of it rose the *Mjollnir*, a splinter of wood riding a splash of flame that was yellow and incredibly bright, brighter than the sun. The noise was a deep rumble that shook the ground and made my chest vibrate, and then, as the rocket rose into the air, a series of crackles and bangs, shock waves like thunderclaps in the air above me.

People were shouting and cheering, and I found myself crying.

I can't describe it. You had to *be* there.

'By all the gods, little Valkyrie!'

*'Thyri, it's working!'*

Thyri could see Norrland laid out like an illuminated map. Clouds were scattered like raindrops over the land.

'She was above the clouds, higher than a bird.'

A blue arc entered the top of the picture, framed by

blackness. *'Thyri,'* said Metaphor. *'That's the horizon. You're so high you can see the curve of the planet. Are you all right?'*

The world was a ball and she had been hurled away like a stone.

She wasn't prepared for this, despite all Metaphor's explanations. Her mind twisted away, seeking refuge.

'Numinus.' She repeated the name like an incantation. 'Numinus.'

Nothing else mattered.

'Yes, Metaphor. I'm all right.'

But now the rocket shook as if slapped. The landscape slid sideways.

'Metaphor?'

*'I was afraid of this. Thyri, the propellant isn't burning evenly. Pehaps the granule packing was disturbed during the launch.'*

Blackness closed around Thyri's vision. 'Metaphor,' she ground out. 'Tell me what I have to do.'

*'We use the attitude thrusters. Touch pad one.'*

Thyri did so. She heard a distant hiss. A cloud of steam obscured her view. The shrinking landscape floated back to the centre of the screen.

Metaphor said, *'Hold it there while I count. One, two, three, four, five. Release. Good.'*

'Has it worked?'

*'Wait while I check ...'* Metaphor's voice tailed away. *'See for yourself.'*

The landscape in the viewer winked away, to be replaced by a star field. Through the familiar constellations crawled a single vagrant star.

'It's Numinus,' Thyri breathed.

*'Yes. Thyri, I think you're going to—'*

Suddenly the ship shuddered.

Roiling gas swept across the field. Numinus's ship drifted from view.

'Metaphor?'

*'Thyri, the hull's failed!'*

Now the monitor showed Thyri the length of the

cylinder. Fire twisted from a wide rip in the side. Metal hoops twisted in white flame.

The cabin's heat grew hellish.

Thyri held her gloved fist over the control panel. 'Tell me what to do, Valkyrie.'

'*Thyri, the hull has failed. It was a good try, but the materials just weren't strong enough. The attitude jets don't have the capacity to compensate for this—*'

'I'm not giving up yet, Valkyrie! Which panel?'

'*Number three!*'

Thyri slammed down her fist. Steam shrieked.

Metaphor shouted, '*On my count … three, four, five, six. Release. Thyri, release the pad now. Thyri!*'

The star field stayed empty. 'I don't see Numinus.' Thyri kept her hand on the control.

'*Thyri, that steam boiler is a box of pig iron. It can't take this. Release!*'

Thyri kept her fist in place. The boiler growled. The heat was unbearable.

At last, the moving star returned to the centre of the screen. Now it showed a spindle form, tumbling slowly.

It was the Sky Longboat, what Metaphor had called the Search Engine.

Thyri released the button. She studied her ship through her viewer.

*Mjollnir's* casing was breached in a dozen places. Fire-hosed into space. Molten iron rained from the hull. The walls of the cabin began to glow a soft red.

'*I'm sorry, Thyri,*' Metaphor said. '*I guess the technology just wasn't up to it.*'

'I'm not dead yet, Metaphor.'

'*I'll tell you one thing. You're giving your people down here quite a show.*'

Another slam.

The star field lurched across Thyri's viewer. The rocket seemed to be spinning. Thyri's stomach knotted as she felt herself tumble—

But there, shooting across the screen, was the Search

Engine. It was so close Thyri could see the sparks dancing over its hull!

She howled in triumph.

The glowing Engine filled the viewer—

She hit.

# CHAPTER EIGHTEEN

# INTERCEPTION

*Mjollnir* rammed into the Search Engine's fabric like a fist into wet cloth. It ripped open the hull and crumpled the decks inside.

Then the cabin slammed into a bulkhead, and *Mjollnir* ground to a sudden stop.

The straps fixing Thyri to her chair snapped, and she was thrown forward. She was wadded into the nose of the cabin like a bit of cloth, but her Valkyrie armour turned stiff and filled with a sticky fluid. Somehow it cushioned her.

The viewer failed.

There was an explosion that slammed the cabin forward. Thyri was rattled like a pebble in a skull. It had been the last of the gunpowder which had powered the rocket.

Then it was over. The sudden silence was as shocking as the thunder that had preceded it.

In the stillness, Thyri spoke.

'Metaphor? Can you hear me?'

*'Thyri! You survived all that?'*

Thyri was … floating. She grabbed a jagged edge of cabin wall. The sudden movement caused all the bruises covering her body to protest at once. 'Valkyrie, I am *flying*.'

*'You're in orbit, Thyri! Well, that was hardly the smooth rendezvous I intended you to make, but never mind.'*

Thyri pulled herself out through the cabin wall. It was difficult to move. Her legs dangled, in the way.

The cabin was a mass of glowing metal. It lay in a disc-shaped chamber. Charred remnants on the walls showed Thyri that this had once been the ocean-like swimming room. Through the ripped hull of the Search Engine Thyri could see stars, a crescent of blue sea. Fragments of ice sparkled around her.

*'Thyri, Numinus has to be trying to regain control of the Search Engine. He'll be in the bridge.'*

'Yes.'

Thyri checked her weapons.

Metaphor had provided her with a laser gun. 'Meet the Regent on equal terms,' she'd said. Now Thyri inspected the piece of sculpted Galaxias metal, and let it drift from her hands.

She didn't want strange Galaxias weapons. She would fight as a Viking warrior.

There was an axe strapped to her waist. In one hand she held her sword of the finest Rhineland iron. In the other she held her shield of wood with its central iron boss. All these weapons had belonged to Gunnar, and had been used by him in the many battles he had won – until his last with the monster Numinus.

Wood and iron. The ancient muscles of the Viking. She had no need of Valkyrie trickery.

And this time there would be no mistake.

She clambered to the top of the cabin and, with gritted teeth, kicked away from the wall. She floated through empty space. Metaphor had warned her it would be like this, *free fall* – but to fly like a bird! She felt her breakfast rise in her throat.

And the air was thin, leaking from the rents in the hull that were imperfectly plugged by *Mjollnir*. Soon she was gasping for breath.

She hit the chamber's axis and rebounded, cursing. Her fingers scrabbled over the smooth material, trying to get a grip.

A door dilated. Air swept past Thyri. She hauled herself through into the green-lit spinal corridor. The door irised closed and air returned with a sigh.

Thyri wiped away sweat. 'Metaphor. I'm in the corridor.'

'*Thyri, move,*' Metaphor hissed. '*The collision has knocked the Search Engine out of orbit. You're falling. You have perhaps only minutes.*'

'That will be enough.'

She pulled herself along the corridor and through the door at its end.

She rolled head-over-heels into the control room. She hit the floor and rebounded slightly, her gaze flicking around.

On the walls obsidian panels flared red. Gunnar's Key, the control for this Search Engine, twisted in the air. The control tables were full of whirling sparks.

Numinus was here. He sat facing the door. The expression on the Regent's face changed as slowly as melting ice. Blood flared in the scar across his cheek. 'You! How?'

Thyri grasped her axe.

'I am not your enemy,' said Numinus.

It was enough to make Thyri hesitate. 'Then who?'

'The girl. The monster. *Metaphor.* And all her kind.' He waved a hand. 'Is it true that none of this is real? That your world and mine were *made* by people somewhere beyond the walls of the universe – for their amusement? If that is so we should work together, escape from this place. Find a way to invade the world of these would-be gods, and punish them for their arrogance.'

Thyri considered that. This airy talk of different worlds, of herself as an imagined creature of some machine's fevered dream. She balanced it against the reality of her life: blood, family, honour, and redemption.

'Prepare to meet your gods, Numinus.' And she raised her axe—

But Numinus's hand flew to the forearm controls of his skin-armour.

To Thyri it was like a nightmare repeat of her last clash with Numinus, the same sequence of lost split-seconds. In a moment the deflector field would sparkle and the battle would be lost.

But the Regent's hand hovered, hesitating. There was something new in his dark face. Relief? Regret?

She threw the axe. It flew across the cabin. The blade laid open Numinus's chest.

The Regent's face crumpled. The black eyes grew cold.

Thyri loomed over the body, breathing hard. She pulled her axe from the shattered chest. Numinus had become a *blood eagle*, as had so many of the enemies of the Vikings in the past.

'*Well, Thyri?*' Metaphor sounded tired. The little Valkyrie had no stomach for killing. '*You have won.*'

'Metaphor? I think he let me kill him.'

'*What?*'

'He could have worked his armour. He had time. But he didn't. Why?'

Metaphor laughed mirthlessly. '*In his universe Regents exert great power. But they are also the first servants of Galaxias – of mankind. I guess Numinus lost the balance between power and duty … but he was guilty and confused. Thyri, once he'd hurt your husband he couldn't turn back. But, perhaps part of him was glad you stopped him before he destroyed your world.*'

Thyri stared down at the cooling body for long seconds. Then she reached down and pressed Numinus's eyelids closed with her thumbs.

She turned away and attached her axe once more to her belt. It was over. The pain of Gunnar was gone. Let it be.

The Search Engine shuddered. Obsidian panels glowed ever more brightly.

What now?

Thyri was suddenly aware that she hadn't planned beyond this moment. She knew there was no way to get back to the ground. But she was alive. And she wanted to stay that way.

'Metaphor? What do I do?'

Silence ...

'Metaphor?'

'*Ah,*' Metaphor coughed weakly. '*I'm sorry, Thyri. This has all been too much for me. Study the instrument panels, the control tables. Your armour will show me what you see.*'

Thyri did so.

Metaphor hesitated for long seconds. '*We have a problem, Thyri. Our homemade spaceship did a lot of damage. You can't land the Search Engine. But you can't stay where you are, either. The ship's orbit is decaying fast. You'll burn up in minutes.*'

Thyri floated in the air. A sense of peace settled over her. 'Then it's over.'

'*No, Thyri. Maybe there's a way. Listen. The table to your left. See the pattern of sparks like a pinwheel? Place your palm over it and ...*'

Slowly, hesitantly, Thyri followed Metaphor's instructions. She heard a growl as ancient engines stirred. An obsidian panel lit up with an image of the world.

She was dropping back into that pond of air. Oceans flicked beneath her keel. She was *flying* this Search Engine, she realized with a sudden tremor. But ... where to? 'Metaphor?'

'*You're heading for the Domain Breach at the north pole. If you're lucky, the way to Galaxias will still be open. You'll pass through to stars.*'

'What good will that do?'

'*You can't come home. Thyri,*' Metaphor said gently. '*I'm sorry. This is your one chance. If you survive the transit, press the stud in the belt of your armour. That will activate a distress*' *signal. With good fortune the Empire will pick up the signal. You'll be rescued.'*

Now ice raced beneath the keel of the Search Engine, almost close enough to touch. 'Metaphor, thank you.'

*'You might not thank me later. Galaxias is a tough place.'*

A curtain of darkness, swirling shapes that hurt her eyes, a central place like a hole in the sky beckoned Thyri. The Domain Breach.

'Little Valkyrie. I think—'

*'Goodbye, Thyri.'*

The hole swallowed her.

# CHAPTER NINETEEN

# WORLDS

Like an icicle in spring the Domain Breach, the way between the universes, had grown tenuous and thin.

The Search Engine roared through.

The way collapsed behind it, dissipated like smoke, closed for ever.

After my farewell to Thyri, the Translator fell silent.

I lay in my chair, breathing hard, utterly weary. At the edge of my attention the medical unit bleeped its warning.

How long had I been inside the Web now? Eight hours? Nine? I knew too much Webtime could actually kill me. But there was nothing I could do about it.

I felt content.

Real or not, it didn't seem to matter any more. This was a world of good people. I had done all I could to save them from the evil of Numinus. I had even helped Thyri get to safety, I hoped. Now it was over.

The light in the little house was failing. I knew I ought to move. Find some blankets ...

It grew colder.

The blood seemed to settle in my veins. Peace settled over me, gentle as a parent's touch.

It was almost dark now ... but there, breaking through the blackness, was a soft yellow light.

I was dizzy, losing consciousness. Perhaps it was the Beacons of Galaxias.

I remember smiling and reaching up my hands, before the blackness closed in.

When I opened my eyes again, I was lying on my back in the spare room.

I couldn't move. I was weak as a kitten. Philip was standing over me, calling my name, pulling my Websuit off me. George was there too. He was crying, the little bug.

I made a mental note. I wouldn't let George forget *that* in a hurry.

I smiled and closed my eyes.

And the Search Engine erupted into stars.

Thyri peered at the obsidian panels. No blue world. No familiar constellations.

Just raw stars.

As Metaphor had instructed her, she pressed the stud at her belt and waited.

After a few hours she saw a ship. It was like a huge bird, metal wings outstretched.

There was a soft sigh behind Thyri. She whirled, axe in hand.

A tall tube of light hummed in the air. It collapsed, slow as settling dust. Gradually the form of a man emerged from the mist.

Black armour. A helmet moulded extravagantly into the shape of a bird's head. A face behind a visor that looked ageless, harsh, tired, but not without humour. The stranger barked at Thyri, as if demanding a response. Then he tapped at controls embedded in a chest plate. 'So. Can you understand me now?'

'My name is Thyri.'

The stranger nodded. 'And I am Hal Beora. I am an Independent Free Trader. Perhaps you've heard of me.'

'That's not likely,' Thyri said dryly. 'Are you from the star

Empire?'

Beora frowned. His hands were empty, but Thyri remembered the ring-weapons Numinus had carried, and watched
him carefully.

'No,' he said. 'We oppose the Empire, and all it stands
for.'

Hal Beora pulled himself slowly around Thyri, inspecting
the Viking with brisk glances, briefly surveying the bridge
of the Search Engine. 'Odd,' he murmured. 'Very odd. I've
never seen a ship like this. I suppose you know there's some
sort of burnt tree sticking out of the hull? And as for you ...
Thyri.' He laughed, not cruelly. 'From which fleabag world
did you pick up that skin armour? It doesn't even fit!'

Thyri studied the Trader. This man had the manner of a
leader. Well, Thyri did not choose to be led.

One thing was certain. If this was a representative of this
universe, life here would be new, strange, unpredictable.
And very, very, dangerous.

But Thor would be here, to protect her and make her
strong.

Thyri touched the familiar wood and iron of her axe and
grinned like a wolf. 'That,' she said, 'is a long story.'

# EPILOGUE

So that's the story.

I don't pretend to understand all of it, or to be able to say what it means for us all.

I just know we're all in grave danger.

Maybe it couldn't happen like this again. The International Court in New York is drawing up *sentience laws*. In future it won't be legal to create conscious beings just for the purposes of entertainment, or even science research. And the beings that exist already, like the inhabitants of WebVin, will have the right to continue to exist inside the Web.

It's good to know Ragnar won't come to any more harm.

But remember Numinus's threat.

He was just a phace, but a phace who became aware of what he was, an artificial creature living inside the Web. And he wanted to escape to Realworld, our world, and punish us.

Numinus was a monster. But his anger was real, and he was ingenious. If not for the courage of Thyri, who knows, he might somehow have succeeded! And what then?

And that is only the threat facing us from *inside* the Web. A threat we have created ourselves. But think about this:

Whatever caused the WebCrash came from *outside*.

There are some who say it must have come from a signal from the stars.

Some say that, fantastic as it seems, this was a prelude to some kind of alien invasion – *in electronic form.*

At first They blundered in, only managing to knock over the Web. But maybe in the future They will be more precise, more deliberate.

If They are real, They are probably learning fast. Because They are here.

I don't know if it's true. All I know is that nothing is impossible. None of the rules apply any more. None of the safety checks.

The human race is in danger.

This isn't a game. Spin back into the Web only if you are prepared, and if you dare.

The Web is a war zone now.

# WEBSPEAK – A GLOSSARY

**AI**
Artificial intelligence. Computer programs that appear to show intelligent behaviour when you interact with them.

**avatar or realoe**
Personas in the Web that are the representations of real people.

**basement-level**
Of the lowest level possible. Often used as an insult, as in 'You've got a basement-level grasp of the situation.'

**bat**
The moment of transition into the Web or between sites. You can 'do a bat' or 'go bat'. Its slang use has extended to the everyday world. 'bat' is used instead of 'come in', 'take a bat' is a dismissal. (From *Blue And Tone*.)

**bite**
To play a trick, or to get something over on someone.

**bootstrap**
Verb, to improve your situation by your own efforts.

**bot**
Programs with AI.

**chasing the fade**
Analysing what has happened in the Web after you have left it.

**cocoon**
A secret refuge. Also your bed or own room.

**cog**
Incredibly boring or dull. Initially specific to the UK and America this

slang is now in use worldwide. (From *Common Or Garden* spider.)

**curl up**  'Go away, I don't like you!' (From *curl up and die*.)

**cyberat**  A Web construct, a descendent of computer viruses, that infests the Web programs.

**cybercafe**  A place where you can get drinks and snacks as well as renting time in the Web.

**cyberspace**  The visual representation of the communication system which links computers.

**d-box**  A data-box; an area of information which appears when people are in Virtual Reality (VR).

**download**  To enter the Web without leaving a Realworld copy.

**down the plug**  A disaster, as in 'We were down the plug'.

**egg**  A younger sibling or annoying hanger-on. Even in the first sense this is always meant nastily.

**eight**  Good (a spider has eight legs).

**flame**  An insult or nasty remark.

**fly**  A choice morsel of information, a clue, a hint.

**funnel**  An unexpected problem or obstacle.

**gag**  Someone, or something, you don't like very much, who you consider to be stupid. (From *Glove And Glasses*.)

**glove and glasses**  Cheap but outdated system for experiencing Virtual Reality. The glasses allow you to see VR, the gloves allow you to pick things up.

**Id**  Interactive display nodule.

**mage**  A magician.

| | |
|---|---|
| **mip** | Measure of computer power. |
| **nick or alias** | A nickname. For example, 'Metaphor' is the nickname of Sarah. |
| **one-mip** | Of limited worth or intelligence, as in 'a one-mip mind'. |
| **phace** | A person you meet in the Web who is not real; someone created by the software of a particular site or game. |
| **phreak** | Someone who is fanatical about virtual reality experiences in the Web. |
| **protocol** | The language one computer uses to talk to another. |
| **raid** | Any unscheduled intrusion into the Web; anything that forces someone to leave; a program crash. |
| **realoe** | See *avatar*. |
| **Realworld** | What it says; the world outside the Web. Sometimes used in a derogatory way. |
| **scuttle** | Leave the Web and return to the Realworld. |
| **silky** | Smarmy, over enthusiastic, untrustworthy. |
| **six** | Bad (an insect has six legs). |
| **slows, the** | The feeling that time has slowed down after experiencing the faster time of the Web. |
| **spider** | A web construct. Appearing in varying sizes and guises, these are used to pass on warnings or information in the Web. The word is also commonly applied to teachers or parents. |
| **spidered-off** | Warned away by a spider. |
| **spin in** | To enter the Web or a Website. |
| **spin out** | To leave the Web or a Website. |

| | |
|---|---|
| **SFX** | Special effects. |
| **strand** | A gap between rows of site skyscrapers in Webtown. Used to describe any street or road or journey. |
| **suck** | To eat or drink. |
| **supertime** | Parts of the Web that run even faster than normal. |
| **TFO** | Tennessee Fried Ostrich. |
| **venomous** | Adjective; excellent; could be used in reference to piece of equipment (usually a Websuit) or piece of programming. |
| **vets** | Veterans of any game or site. Ultra-vets are the *crème de la crème* of these. |
| **VR** | Virtual Reality. The illusion of a three dimensional reality created by computer software. |
| **warlock** | A sorcerer; magician. |
| **Web** | The worldwide network of communication links, entertainment, educational and administrative sites that exists in cyberspace and is represented in Virtual Reality. |
| **Web heads** | People who are fanatical about surfing the Web. (See also phreaks.) |
| **Web round** | Verb; to contact other Web users via the Web. |
| **Websuit** | The all over body suit lined with receptors which when worn by Web users allows them to experience the full physical illusion of virtual reality. |
| **Webware** | Computer software used to create and/or maintain the Web. |
| **widow** | Adjective; excellent; the term comes from the Black Widow, a particularly |

poisonous spider.

**wipeout**    To be comprehensively beaten in a
Web game or to come out worse in
any Web situation.

# OTHER BOOKS IN
# THE WEB SERIES

**GULLIVERZONE** by Steve Baxter

February 7, 2027, World Peace Day. It's a day of celebration everywhere. Even access to the Web is free today. It's the chance Sarah's been waiting for, a chance to sample the most wicked sites, to visit mind-blowing virtual worlds. She chooses GulliverZone and the chance to be a giant amongst the tiny people of Lilliput.

But the peace that is being celebrated in the real world does not extend into cyberspace. There is a battle for survival being fought in Lilliput and what Sarah discovers there in one day will be enough to change her life for ever – providing she can get out to live it …

GULLIVERZONE, the fear is anything but virtual.

GULLIVERZONE ready for access.

FEEL UP TO ANOTHER?
**DREAMCASTLE** by Stephen Bowkett

Dreamcastle is the premier fantasy role-playing site on the Web, and Surfer is one of the premier players. He's one of the few to fight his way past the 500th level, one of the few to take on the Stormdragon and win. But it isn't enough, Surfer had his eyes on the ultimate prize. He wants to be the best, to discover the dark secret at the core of Dreamcastle.

And he's found the girl to take him there. She's called Xenia and she's special, frighteningly special.

He's so obsessed that he's blind to Rom's advice, to Kilroy's friendship and to the real danger that lies at the core of the Dreamcastle. A danger that could swallow him whole … for real.

DREAMCASTLE, it's no fantasy.

DREAMCASTLE ready for access.

## THINK YOU'RE UP TO IT?
**UNTOUCHABLE** by Eric Brown

Life might be easier for most people in 2027 but for Ana Devi, whose only home is the streets of New Delhi, it's a battle for survival. She's certainly never dreamed of visiting the bright virtual worlds of the Web. And when her brother is kidnapped the Web is certainly the last thing she is thinking about. But the Web holds the secret to what has happened to her brother and to dozens of other New Delhi street children.

How can Ana possibly find enough money to access the Web when she can barely beg enough to eat each day? Who will help her when her caste means that no one will even touch her? Somehow she must find a way or she will never see her brother again.

Dare you touch the truth of UNTOUCHABLE?

UNTOUCHABLE ready for access.

## TAKE ANOTHER WALK ON THE WILD SIDE
**SPIDERBITE** by Graham Joyce

In 2027 a lot of schooltime is Webtime. Imagine entering Virtual Reality and creeping through the Labyrinth with the roars of the Minotaur echoing in your ears? Nowhere near as dull as the classroom. The sites are open to all, nothing is out of bounds. So why has Conrad been warned off the Labyrinth site? There shouldn't be any secrets in Edutainment.

Who is behind the savage spiders that swarm around Conrad whenever he tries to enter the site? And why do none of his friends see them? There is a dark lesson being taught at the centre of the Labyrinth ...

SPIDERBITE, school was never meant to be this scary ...

SPIDERBITE ready for access.

## ARE YOU READY TO GO AGAIN?
**LIGHTSTORM** by Peter F. Hamilton

Ghostly lights out on the marsh have been the subject of tales and rumours for as long as anyone can remember but the reality is far more frightening than any ghost story. Something is going wrong at the nearby energy company and they are trying to keep it a secret. Somebody needs to be told. But Aynsley needs help to do it. The Web keeps him in touch with a network of friends across the world and it might just offer him a way in past the company security to find out exactly what's going on.

But the Web works both ways. If Aynsley can get to the company then the company can get to him. And the company has a way of dealing with intruders.

LIGHTSTORM, sometimes it's best to be in the dark.

LIGHTSTORM ready for access.

## IS THIS THE END?
**SORCERESS** by Maggie Furey

A fierce and menacing intelligence is corrupting the very heart of the Web. Vital research data is being stolen. Someone or something is taking control of a spectacular new game zone. The Web is no longer safe. The Sorceress continues to outwit all who attempt to destroy her, but her time is running out and she will stop at nothing to get what she wants. Someone must stop her.

Only one person has the power to overcome the awesome creator of the Web.

But who could survive a battle with the Sorceress?

SORCERESS ready for access.

## JUST WHEN YOU THOUGHT IT WAS SAFE ...
**CYDONIA** by Ken Macleod

Who can you trust in a world full of conspiracy? Links and Weaver used to be bitter game zone rivals in the Web but they are forced to rely on each other when the lies and deceit surrounding the Cydonia conspiracy site begin to spread into the outside world. If you believed everything you'd end up trusting no-one. Caught up in their own tangled web no-one is looking to where the real story is; the stars.

CYDONIA, the truth is nowhere.

CYDONIA, ready for access September 1998.

## TRY THIS ONE FOR SIZE
**COMPUTOPIA** by James Lovegrove

There's a rival system to the Web; the Net. It's faster, the effects are better, the sites are cooler. It should be the answer to everyone's dreams. So why is Jerry's dad, the man who invented it, acting like it's a nightmare? Jerry has to find out. But the only way he can do that is to access the Net and his dad has forbidden him ever to do that. But with the help of his friend, Flygirl, Jerry breaks all the rules and discovers something that is just out of this world.

COMPUTOPIA, perfection is a dangerous thing.

COMPUTOPIA, ready for access December 1998.

A WHITE KNUCKLE RIDE
**SPINDRIFT** by Maggie Furey

Why has an old enemy come back to haunt Cat and Eleni?
And should they trust a warning from someone that evil?
Soon they have no choice as the threat that has haunted
their dreams spills over into the Web. Is Realworld next? Bit
by bit the story falls into place and the girls find out that
their world doesn't just belong to them. And when that
happens there really is no place to hide.

SPINDRIFT, nowhere to run to.

SPINDRIFT, ready for access December 1998